AF001761

Tall Tales:

THE VERSE OF JOHN ALBERT BEST

Tall Tales:

THE VERSE OF JOHN ALBERT BEST

Copyright remains the property of John Best © 2019

All rights reserved. No part of this book may be reproduced, stored in a retrieval system, or transmitted, in any form or by any means without the prior written permission of the publisher, nor be otherwise circulated in any form of binding or cover other than that in which it is published and without a similar condition being imposed on the subsequent purchaser.

First published in 2019 by Long John Best in association with Bent Banana Books

Email longjohnbest@bigpond.com

Email bentbananabooks@gmail.com

A CiP catalogue record for this book is available from the Australian National Library.

ISBN: 978-0-9805684-2-4(paperback)

Cover graphic by Carolyne Morris

Cover design: Ian Curr

Foreword by LJB

Readers, please be warned some poems are a bit rough and may offend, while others may lift and delight. Life's like that. We can't live our lives in a comfort bubble, and why would we want to? Growth and comfort cannot co-exist. Knowledge dispels fear, so face your demons and later, you will wonder what you worried about. Life is for living, get into it. Give it a go, don't die wondering.

This book is a result of twenty years of dabbling with rhyme and meter. I enjoyed putting it together, hope you gain some insight or joy from it too. I dedicate this book to my family, my mentor, the late Milton Taylor, and other poets for their assistance down the years, as well as Zoe Younger and Bernie Dowling for their urging and assistance.

Long John Best, 2019

All errors, omissions or lack of grammar have been acquired since leaving school.

Profits from the sale of this book go to RSPCA QLD.

Contents

Tasha, a Gift of a Dog 6
The Vet 7
Tasha Departing 8
Irrelevant 9
Now and Then 10
Have You Forgotten, They Don't Forgive 12
Present, not Correct (or A Mother's Day Gift Gone Wrong) 14
P Plates 16
Is Money a Religion? 17
It's All Relative 18
The Cricket 20
Stranger at the Door 21
Perceptions 22
Henry's Passing 23
My Heart Is Tranquil Now 24
One April Day 25
Don't Ever Mention His Name 26
Can't Win 27
Feet of Clay 28
Who Can We Trust? 28
Misunderstood Man 29
A Positive Attitude 29
Risk Assessment 29
Family Trilogy 30
My Family 30
Family Ties 30
Christmas Keeps Our Family Strong 31
The Butch Truckerman 32
Horse Sense 34
Should I Have Rescued This Dog? 35
Assassins 35
I'm a Lucky Son of Me Mum 36
Are the Elderly Revolting? 38
Robbie Rabbit 40
On Our Election 41
The Good Drum 42
Devious Devils 43
Forget Mondays 44
St Don, the good butcher of Petrie 46
Driving Hazards 48
Our Big Day Out 49
It Pays to Listen 50
It's All in the Mind, I Think 52
Hello Dolly 54
What's Fair 56
Forever Overdue 57
Verandah Dreaming 58
How the Orient Express 60
Found at Last the AE1 60

HMAS AE2 The Silent Anzac	61
Saying Grace is Saying Thank You	62
A Tale of Two Wolves	64
A Birthday over Brisbane	64
Freddy, a Prince of a Frog	65
Banking on a Friend	65
Paddy's Lament.	66
I Wonder	66
Birds of a Feather	66
Break of Day the Westfield Way	68
Luigi	70
The Deodorant Stick	70
Fido, my Friend	71
The Worst Two Hundred Dollars I Never Saved	72
Murder, He Wrote	74
Cheap Flights. Honesty Don't Pay	76
Cuckoo Land	76
Back When	77
Dog Food Diet	77
When Irish ears aren't smiling	78
Let's put some fun in funeral ads	78
What are you here after? I know	79
The RFDS (Donations required)	79
Israel	80
Perspectives	80
Hotel Letter	81
Mad with the Power	82
Ambition and Capability	82
The Painted Horse	84
The Pillars	84
Railway? What Railway?	85
The Interview	86
Glorious to Behold	86
Our family are close	87
There's Something in the Air	88
I Didn't Wanna	90
The Procedure or Overreaction	91
Lost Luggage	92
You Just Dunno	93
Roses Are Blooming, Why Pick on Me?	94
The Queue	95

This is the story of an uninvited visitor to our Home who stayed for fifteen years. She proved herself to be a wonderful warm and loyal companion. Honest and non-judgmental she was a great listener. We loved her then as we love her still.

Tasha, a Gift of a Dog

A puppy's paw print, placed in concrete, nearly forty years ago,
I was dirty when she did it, but no more, how could I know?
Now, every time I see it, takes me back, to reminisce
'Bout them two young girls, who lived here, 'bout Old Tasha, I still miss.

She came; a gift we did not want, a golden fluffy ball.
We had Samantha, six months old; no love to spare, at all,
Or so we thought, but as dogs do, they creep inside your heart,
And when our Kylie came along, it was much too late to part.

Two darling daughters and their mate, they were like them Musketeers,
They were all for one and one for all, we never held no fears,
A snake would maybe take them or perhaps they'd wind up drowned.
No, you'd never entertain the thought, while Tasha was around.

She was like some hairy shadow; she'd not let them out of sight.
She'd cry, when they went off to school, but the welcome home at night,
She'd be leaping, barking, grinning, and though some may think us daft,
We all swore, when they got back from camp, that big old dog, she laughed.

Oh! The years, fly by so swiftly, young girls grow, move out, and wed,
Too soon their kids were wiggling, giggling, snuggling in our bed.
Then I'd walk 'em up the driveway, to the spot where Tasha trod,
Tell 'em tales of two Princesses, and their dog who's gone to God.

Then I'd show 'em where she's buried, by the fence, in our back yard.
"Gramps how come she's here and up there too?" it all got far too hard.
So, I promptly changed the subject, and I herd them all inside,
And show 'em photos of their Mums, from babyhood to bride.

But old Tasha kept appearing, and it soon became a game,
They'd flick quickly through the pictures, 'til they'd spot her, shout her name,
They'd cry, "Tasha, Tasha, Tasha," like their Mothers used to call,
And I'd half expect Old Tasha, to come flashing down the hall.

Slipping, scratching at the polished boards, she'd let out her worried bark,
Yeah, wherever you look 'round our place, old Tasha's left her mark.
Three great mates, who grew together, sadly one grew old too fast,
Wasn't easy, telling young girls why such friendships cannot last.

I grow older, tears come quicker, hindsight wisdom's far too late.
I shoulda told you that I loved you more, while you were here, old mate,
There's a green patch in our paddock, that I talk to when I mow,
And a puppy's paw print, set in concrete, nearly forty years ago.

Inspired by a piece called A Dog's Purpose. Anonymous.

The Vet

Ron and Lisa's dog was Bluey, part Blue Heeler, nearly ten,
Real good mate, more like a brother, to their six-year-old son Ben.
I'm their vet, I've known the family, I dunno, for quite a while,
Watching boy and dog grow closer, one of Life's joys, makes me smile.
Only school days find them parted, faithful friend waits by the gates.
But Life's unfair, cruel. Cancer comes, claws deep and devastates,
And it's now my task to tell them, all their prayers have been in vain,
Euthanasia, only option, to relieve poor Bluey's pain.

Ben had asked if he could be there, which I thought strange for a kid,
But Ron and Lisa had agreed, and I'm so glad that they did.
For not before or ever since, have I witnessed such a scene,
At the passing of a loved one, sort of spiritual, I mean.
He seemed so calm when patting Blue, who looked up and licked Ben's tears,
Respect and love and dignity, shown way, far beyond the years
Of their short lives spent together, then we sat and wondered why,
Bad humans live a long, long, time, and good dogs too soon must die.

Then Ben spoke, "I know the answer." He is six what would he say?
He gave us words of wisdom, that I dwell on to this day.
"Most people have to learn to live, a good life, to love, be kind,
To be nice to one another, and I think that you will find,
That this really is the reason, but I'm six I could be wrong,
See dogs already know that stuff, so don't have to stay as long."

Tasha Departing

The more years you tuck behind you, the more memories you get,
And, by gee, I've had some great ones, far more good than I regret.
Yet there's one that still upsets me, comes to haunt me now and then,
The day we put our Tasha down. I can still remember when
Paul The Vet said, "John it's time, mate, say goodbye she has to go."
All our family in denial, we just didn't want to know.
This the third time he had told us, we discussed it and agreed,
We would love her all that weekend, and on Monday, do the deed.

Faithful Tasha, sat and watched me, as I dug that great big hole,
Where we'd lay her worn out body, but no grave could hold her soul.
The girls hugged her Monday morning, like she'd not been hugged before,
Tear filled cries of, "Please don't leave us," as they closed the school bus door.
Tash sat watching from our back seat, grand old lady full of grace,
Framed there in the rear-view mirror, she see Judas in my face?
Eight a.m. we're in the car park, the receptionist ran out,
Her first morning, eager, friendly, "what's this visit all about?"

Glenny bawled, "She's being put down." They clung crying 'neath a tree.
My mind said you must take her in, my heart said let her be.
She stands trembling on the table, don't you tell me dogs don't know.
I hold her close, she snuggles in, terrified I'll let her go.
She gazes up into my eyes, fifteen years of trust lay there,
And what happened next I tell, was almost too much to bear.
As the needle's contents entered, she relaxed, and just before she died,
Did she forgive me for my treachery? When she licked, the tears I'd cried.

There is a vast difference socially between the ages of 15 and 30. This diminishes as the young grow older. As an apprentice in the Airforce our instructors had seen service in World war two and Korea, this created an enormous gulf in experience. However, when they returned to general duties and we were finding our way in the service, the gap reduced and we became friends. On leaving the service these ties were maintained. Friendship is a bit like owning a dog, you've got to take it for a walk now and again, so I'd ring them up and see how they were going. Lately I had noticed a dropping off in their attitudes to "nobody loves me or wants or needs what I know. "Was this self-pity, will I wind up this way or am I already there? Thus, I wrote the following. I hope it has some relevance for you. I called it, strangely enough

Irrelevant

"I'm irrelevant, that's what I am," my old mate said to me,
When I asked him" how yer going?" and I thought, how could that be,
Him the bloke that I looked up to like a father me the son,
Him who taught me most of what I know, how could he come undone?
He was competent and vital, goer, him the one who dares.
Now dejected and despondent, 'cause he says "nobody cares."
Says "nobody gives a rat's arse 'bout the likes of me and you,
It's all bottom line and market share and stock-chips that are blue.
They're obsessed with bloody money, gotta have more than they need.
If there's one thing stuffing up this world, it's all this flaming greed.
Makes you wonder why we listened when they played their call to arms,
Why we left the factories, offices the railway and the farms.
Why we marched like bloody lemmings to the slaughter into hell,
To the symphony of mortar, mortal screams and bloody shell.
We meant money, mate, and power, to them mongrels at the top.
Oh, Jesus, get a load of me, I think I'd better stop,
Before I have a heart attack, and topple off me perch,
No, I haven't got no answers, you'd better go and search
Down among them politicians not with me, with half a brain.
Could you go another cuppa mate, now when's it gunna rain?"
So, we shared another cuppa then I left him sitting there,
An old digger disempowered, with a disillusioned stare.
And I dwelt on what he'd told me, 'bout the lies that they'd been fed,
Of his cobbers he'd not heard from, so he figured they were dead,
Bout the loss of their potential, to contribute to our land,
Fed like fodder to the cannons, good blokes wasted out of hand.
Why for Chrissake why? I question, does it still go on to-day,
There are other Gods than money, there must be a better way.

I'm guilty, like most people, of whinging instead of counting our blessings, that we live at a great time in such a great country as Australia. Hence the following, I've called it, Now and Then. This is an adaptation of a poem I presented when the Transport Department hosted a seminar for the Union of Publique Transport

Now and Then

Gee I'm jack of all those jokers who complain about the drive
From Sydney say to Brisbane, who claim they're tired, when they arrive.
Struth, our roads were never better, motor cars the best they've been,
Spare a thought for those first settlers, when they lobbed on the scene.

The locals all went walkabout, those on water used canoes,
So, they'd not a lot of options, from which they had to choose.
Late in the Eighteenth Century was when this land first feels,
The plodding gait of bullocks and the heavy weight of wheels.

We had no roads prepared for this, for we'd no place to go,
We laid some down round Sydney Town, but us convicts we'd work slow.
As our population increased, we began to make a push.
To North and South and out we went, all heading for the Bush.

The going rough, but folk were tough, back in those early days,
And our dreams relied on bullocks strong; to pull our two wheeled drays.
Them drivers, they could turn a phrase, and I swear that this is true,
'Twas the language used by bullockies, that made our skies so blue.

In the early Eighteen Hundreds, coach lines started to expand,
Now horse drawn, out of village, towns, they moved across this land.
But roadless regions took their toll, springs sprung and axles broke,
Then Freeman Cobb took up the bit, produced his masterstroke.

Imported coaches from the States, slung low on straps of leather,
His big red monsters rode the ruts, day night, in any weather.
He'd not compete with new laid rail; he'd fill in, in between,
Was his transport integrated? Yes, I think it might have been.

Came the middle of the nineteenth, she was on for young and old,
This new colony was struggling, but then we found it: Gold.
Scattered right across this country, in places God forsook,
So, we had to go and get it, had to go and have a look.

Needing towns and infrastructure, Diggers needing to be fed,
Needing grog and entertainment, Diggers waiting to be bled.
We used pushbikes, donkeys, camels, anything to ride or pull,
As if a gold rush weren't enough, then came the bloody wool.

We pushed paddle wheelers up to Bourke, no good if in a hurry,
You just might sit the season out, till Darling greets the Murray.
And all the while the railway lines crept slowly o'er the plains,
And bush folk gathered by the tracks, to cheer the passing trains.
Paper!

Then omnibus and flatbed trucks, appeared on rough bush roads,
And Cobb and Co and carriers, watched as they stole their loads,
Off-shore stand clippers, rigging slack, their sails now sadly furled,
As steam and motor vessels bear their cargoes round the world.

The Twentieth Century has arrived, and we stand on the brink
Of wars, abroad, not on our shores, the world begins to shrink.
For aviators soar aloft, on wood and fabric wings,
Men, magnifique in their machines, begin to do their things.

Transatlantic, then Pacific, flights of fancy, aircrews die,
Now an everyday occurrence, con trails weave across the sky,
Linking lands of different culture, different colour, different creed,
Intercontinental travel, flown at supersonic speed.

So, the next time you go travelling, be it home or overseas,
You remember what you heard to-day, and fellow Aussies please,
Cast your mind back, to those pioneers, who blazed the tracks you take,
Count your blessings, cos compared to theirs, your life's a piece of cake.

*This happened because, to be honest, basically men don't listen to women very well.
Based on a true story from an old neighbour of ours.*

Have You Forgotten, They Don't Forgive

I'm not big, on instructions, I mean listening to, not giving.
I suppose I'll have to change my ways, if I'm to go on living,
With this woman, Missy Perfect, who in turn blights, lights my life,
The all-powerful, all knowing, she knows nuffing, Glen my wife.

'Twas our daughters eighteenth birthday, a significant event,
Seems a cake, was ordered paid for, and myself was duly sent,
With instructions, quite specific, most of which I had not heard,
'Cept for Kylie, cake, it's paid for, paid, to Scrooge, the magic word.

Then My Luck, she chucked a lefty, when she shoulda gone straight on.
We boast two bakers, in our town, to the wrong one, I had gone.
Then my cactus Karma, she kicked in, two surnames spelt the same,
Did that cakeshop sheila cop it; "you've stuffed up her Christian name."

"'Stead of Kylie you've got Karen, you insensitive fat cow,
I've paid top dollar for this cake; you bloody fix it now."
Which they did, but weren't too happy, I heard, bully, mongrel, pig,
And that made me feel, much macho, you don't mess with Mr Big.

But euphoria flew out the door, on entering our kitchen.
What's this? Where did you get it? That's not ours, and other bitching.

So, I ruefully returned it, with apologies profound,
Those bakehouse ladies nodded lots, but uttered not a sound.
I suspect my missus rang 'em, and became sure of that, when,
As I shuffled shamefaced from the shop to a chorus of; Ahh Men.

Then I had to front the other mob, and don't bad news, travel quick,
I was greeted with, Here's Mr Head, and How yer going Dick?
They never let up, do they; cripes, you make just one mistake,
And every Birthday ever since, it's Oh Dad'll get the cake.

Now, instructions are handwritten notes, which I've forgot to bring,
Christ that happened twenty years ago, seems I've not learnt a thing.

Cheap Flights. Honesty don't Pay

I was fiddling with the thingo, which I haven't mastered yet,
All I know is I'm the curser, when I'm on the internet.
Then the room filled with her perfume, just a towel hid her delights,
When she asked me what I'm doing, I said "Searching for cheap flights."
I'd not seen her behaving, in the manner that she did,
I'm not lying, comes on Cougar, like she wants another kid.
Never ever shown such passion, muttered ja da dore,
Like the mounting yard at Randwick, she's now got me on the floor,
Ripping tearing at me clothing, I grew fearful for me parts.
But her lust soon turned to loathing,
"Whoa, whoa," says I, "These cheap flights are for me darts."

This next one is written for that second Sunday in May, so beloved by retail outlets everywhere.

Present, not Correct (or A Mother's Day Gift Gone Wrong)

I'd lost my Mum, some time ago, the one who gave me life,
Time to focus on the next, in line, my poor long-suffering wife.
I've not been a great gift giver, no I better take that back,
I never give nobody nuffing, the Missus yells, "You're slack,
You are miserable and lousy, poor excuse you, for a man,
And they're all your good points, Mongrel." Can you tell she's not a fan?

But I'm not mean, just careful, and before my stocks get lower,
I'll try and buy her something nice, a second-hand lawn mower.
New plug and blades, a touch of paint, gift wrapped, and all degreased,
But is she happy: no not her: Dame Ingrate, is not pleased.
Then she claims, that she can't start it, can I come and lend a hand,
I says, woman you are joking, I am off to golf, as planned.

I get home, a little worse for wear, and you won't believe it, mate,
There's Sarcastic Scissors, clipping grass, from the front door to the gate,
Alcohol has made me bold, though left me short of clever,
I should have praised the job she'd done, not scoffed at her endeavour,
By giving her a toothbrush, then giggling, falling in a heap,
Saying, soon as you clean the lawn up, love, the driveway needs a sweep?

It's not difficult, in hindsight, to tell what a bride'll do,
When she's ridiculed, belittled, she'll turn homicidal, true!
With her scissors and my toothbrush, and her steel capped wellies on,
Any future hopes of breeding, let me tell you are well gone.
I can see now why a cyclone should be named after a girl,
I have seen the blood lust in her eyes, I have watched the dervish whirl.

Three weeks I spent in ICU, just for my sight, to clear,
While Lady Muck, she mows in style, on a big brand new, John Deere.
And Me, I've learnt to zip my lip, but no way am I a whimp.
I'm back playing golf three days a week, but I'll always have the limp.
So, Is marriage a relationship? Seems to me it's all a joke,
Cos, it only works if one is right, but then the one who's left's, a bloke.

I wrote this to try to slow down the senseless road deaths of our young people. Young people who are on the threshold of life. They have been nurtured and loved, to get to this stage, they have taken on board an education, to enable them to make their way in this wonderful world, only to see it thrown away needlessly, for what.

P Plates

Heading home from, doesn't matter, driven further than makes sense,
When this car, coming towards me, leaves the road, ploughs through a fence.
Hits a tree, this far above ground, then explodes, disintegrates.
I pull up, you have to, don't cha, might be me, could be me mates.

I run back, I'm far from certain, not too keen on what I'll find,
While *'s not my problem, do not get involved*, keeps running through my mind.
And the sight I see before me, is not one that I'll forget,
And the fact I couldn't help at all, still fills me with regret.

Five, yeah five, lay in and round the wreck, all gone, I stood there, numb,
Settling dust and eerie silence, broken by a cry for, "Mum."
One survivor, it's the driver, makes you wonder, don't it though.
Didn't let on 'bout the others, didn't think he'd wanna know.

I held him close but gentle, ambulance wailing through the night,
Though he'd still not asked about his friends, I think he knew all right.
I feel, I felt his soul departing, as he let go, his last breath,
"Tell their parents I'm so sorry." Then he passed, from life to death.

But does "I'm so sorry, cut it?" It's a feeble, weak excuse,
For five families that are gutted, no, it's not much bloody use.
Never, ever, can they be the same, though their demeanour's brave,
Their sense of loss, their sadness, they will carry to their grave.

Kids, a Life is not some kind of game, that you switch off or on.
Sure, you can turn it off all right, just once, and then it's gone
For ever. Think, before you drink or drive, and never mix the two,
Or this story you just heard from me, may one day feature you.

Forgive me, if I've upset some, I see tears, some eyes are red.
But I'll take upset any day, it's far preferable to, dead.

Is Money a Religion?

Big Jugs Jessie ran a Cathouse, and a mighty fine one too,
Every payday was a goldmine, blocked the footpath with the queue.
Booming business meant expansion, so she started in to build,
Next door neighbour, Reverend Neville, stands to reason, none too thrilled.

Launched a campaign for its closure, frantic praying day and night,
It was Whores versus The Chosen, Fallen women, Righteous Might.
Were those workmen on a bonus? One can only guess at that,
The Grand Opening bang on schedule, two days' time, the House of Cat.

Came a storm, was out of season, rhythmic, cataclysmic sound,
Lit the sky with frightening lightning, burning Jugs Joint to the ground.
How those Holy Rollers hollered, "Let those sinners taste the sword."
All the salivating zealots claimed, "A victory for the Lord."

The parishioners, all smugness, bragged aloud, "The power of prayer,"
Til a letter from Jugs' lawyer left them gasping in despair.
She'd sued Church and Congregation, 'For the downfall of my place,
By direct or divine action', put this way, she had a case.

The Church spun, through one eighty, and 'most vehemently denies,
All or part in escalating this bad building's sad demise'.
The Judge read both depositions, then was seen to scratch his head,
Looked from plaintiff to defendant, then he stood and smiling said,

"Seems we have a whorehouse madam, who gives prayer a great big wrap,
And a church and congregation, who've decided praying's crap",
Solomon called both to His Chambers, leaving neither in the lurch,
Saw Jess's new Cathouse rise from ashes, her Silent Partner, Rev Nev's Church.

Our Good mate Jack Drake wrote a very funny poem called The Cattle Dog's Revenge. The only complaint I had was that he claimed city relatives lobbed up at his place with half a loaf of bread and a couple of stubbies, hung around for a month and, thought they were doing him a favour. This has not been my, experience, far from it, so I wrote this to square up the ledger. I suspect farmers need a good sense of humour or are masochists, preferably both, to soldier on as they do. So, don't take this to heart.

It's All Relative

They're un-bloody-believable, Dad's voice almost a sob,
As he gently puts the phone down, and sez to Mum, Your Mob,
Would test the patience of a saint, and Christ knows I'm not one,
They'll be back down here to morrer, "We're just coming for a run,
We've some business in the City, don't youse go to, too much fuss
Cos you know we're only family, and there's just the six of us."

Just six colossal carnivores; I watch Dad's shoulders drop,
As he contemplates the purchase of the local butcher shop,
And a hotel wouldn't go astray, I hear him whinge to Mum,
Can we get you all a cuppa? "No, all we drink is rum."
But do they bring the keg they'll drain? Not on your bloody life.
Just your brother and his offspring, and that door mat that's his wife.

And what offspring, off the planet, there's no gap between their eyes,
If their IQ topped their boot size, it'd be a big surprise.
"Oh they've all attended private schools, cos we've a Family Trust",
With concessions that we couldn't get Dad mutters in disgust,
And do they offer any money? No, you'd get more off a thief,
"Jeez we'd love to leave you something, but see we're on drought relief."

Dad ponders if them Pollies, when they're chucking that about,
Spare a thought for city rellies, who must also suffer drought
The only time we get relief is when they're trapped by flood,
Dad sez water now is thicker they can stick their bloody blood.
And they'll be back down for the EKKA, that'll last more than a week
By now Dad's face is crimson and he finds it hard to speak.

That CS bloody IRO should declare them all a pest,
When they descend on city folk, like locusts from the West.
So he shot them off a letter, their response was pretty vague,
They claimed in sufficient numbers and that six was not a plague,
Well Dad blew his stack and rang 'em back, he swore and screamed and fumed,
Anyone of these you'd call a plague if you saw what they consumed.

Mum's got him on the Valium, he seems much quieter now,
But them Bundy Ads excite him and he bristles at a cow,
We don't mention Landed Gentry, least not when Dad's about,
We sometimes talk of flood and rain but never speak of drought,
And the EKKA, she's a no-no, hears the word and he'll burr up,
And Mum's never ever told Dad, they'd a starter in the Cup.

Oh they talk of town and country, and how the twain should meet,
But World War Three looks likely, should Akubras grace our street,
So Mum's selling up our little Home, sez it causes too much stress,
Bought a Four-wheel drive and caravan, we'll have no fixed address,
We'll just stooge around the coastline, and avoid the city's push,
We'll be unemployed but no more annoyed, by those Bastards from the Bush.

This one came about when I was out on our back verandah and I saw this little cricket, one of those ugly little critters with the big claws. As soon as I picked it up I was immediately carried back to my childhood when someone gave me one to hold. I remember I nearly cacked myself. It didn't hurt at all, just gently pushed against my fingers to try to get away. It prompted me to write the first verse of this and then Glenny, my beloved critic, said that that was a really nice poem and I should try to weave it into some kind of a lifestyle effort. Here it is, called:

The Cricket

Hold it gentle, not too tightly, that's a Cricket in your hand.
I still feel the magic of it, and I somehow think it's planned,

I pass this feeling on to my kids and they in turn to theirs,
As the tiny claws start pushing, you can see the little hairs

On their necks rise up in wonder: you begin to understand.
Hold it gentle, not too tightly, that's a Life there, in your hand.

Your child's life is, like that Cricket, fleetingly to have and hold.
Hold it gentle, not too tightly, just firm enough to mould

A warm decent human being, one who knows what's right, what's wrong.
Then you'll feel their claws, a pushing, their time's come, to move along.

Turn them loose, give them your blessing, sure they're young, but so were we,
And we know that they may stumble, but that's part of being free.

Someday, should we get lucky, sometime, further down the track,
They may have children of their own, may choose to bring them back

To visit, let us hold them, one more generation, spanned.
Hold it gentle, not too tightly, that's a Grandchild in your hand.

I dream, one day, I'll see their kids, hold their tiny hands in mine.
If that should happen, well and good, but if not, that's also fine.

For I've had my share of fortune, a great family and true friends,
And I sense, somewhere, not far away, is where my journey ends.

I feel the hourglass of my life, sort of running short on sand.
Hold me gentle, not too tightly, lest I'm that Cricket in your hand.

This one arrived in the form of a yarn through cyberspace which I filed away for later. That's usually a time that seldom comes. Fortunately, we had a visit from my daughter and the grandsons who returned from an early morning walk accompanied by a dog who didn't want to leave. This was the catalyst – can you say that about a dog poem? – for:

Stranger at the Door

He just turned up out of nowhere, big wet nose against the screen,
That's the fly-wire not the TV, tiredest dog you ever seen.
He was big and beige and baggy, with a face said, seen it all.
When he smiled, his tail got waggy, as I shuffled down the hall.

Labrador, we'd often longed for, never had the means to own,
Everyone of ours a bitzer, cherished, all gone, we're alone.
Sometimes talk about a puppy, but to us it don't seem fair
To travel, like we hope to, when your best friend can't be there.
Still, I put him out some water, our verandah's cool and wide,
He drank then circled slowly, 'fore collapsing, like he died.

He was plumb wore out, I figured, twitched and snored like old men do.
So I sat and watched him dreaming, that filled in an hour or two.
He woke up, as I grew noddy, licked my hand, then took his leave,
I thought, Jeez, I'm gunna miss you, but I'd not too long to grieve.

For next morning and thereafter, for a fortnight he'd appear,
Though adoption wasn't mentioned, his intentions seemed quite clear.
Everyday the same, siesta, he'd lick, I'd scratch, then off he'd go.
Guilty feelings, owners miss him? Wrote a note to let them know.

Fixed to collar, off he ambled, this could end it all I thought,
But foreboding turned to laughter, with the answer that he brought.
"Pleased to meet you. This is different, Dog Express, that's kind of sweet,
And we thank you for your kindness, seems Pete's landed on his feet.

See our home has seven children, guess he feels he needs a spell,
Come to that I'm overdue one, Monday may I come, as well?"
And she came, we made her welcome, lovely girl we both adore.
While Mary dozes in the hammock, hairy Pete he hugs the floor.
Lonely dogs or lonely people, Life don't have to be that way,
Feeling Friendless, need a soulmate, ring the RSPCA.

There are occasions in your life when you should just stop and take an inventory on how you're travelling. This may well be the first time that you stand on the podium at the tour de France, receive a Victoria Cross, or get any coloured medal at the Olympic Games. Of course, none of these things have happened to me yet. I'm more likely to do a stock take at the birth of a grandchild or a near-death experience or more recently, birthdays ending in zero, of which I've had more than my share. Out of all this navel-gazing came:

Perceptions
The year of living dangerously does not sound, like too much fun,
Seems to me they should be grateful, that they only had the one.
One bad year to me's a bonus, see I've had sixty-seven,
Plus several in a coma, which in hindsight, were like heaven.
I have had things happen to me, at which lesser blokes would cringe,
But if there's one good thing about me, it's, I never goes the whinge.

My first day on earth, I couldn't breathe, so they whacked me on the bum.
I couldn't talk or walk or nothing, I clung onto my Mum.
I never ever had a Dad, 'cos Mum said we was too poor,
But I bear a close resemblance to old Cec who lived next door.
I caught every illness going, spent my childhood fraught with pain,
But if there's one good thing about me, it's, you won't hear me complain.

Then I entered adolescence, truth to tell it entered me,
Overnight I shot up like a weed, till I stood six feet three.
I was gawky, stalky, dorky; I was all of that and more,
I'd go to bed at half past ten, and by dawn be six foot four.
I was one long living sinew, like some virus overgrown,
But if there's one good thing about me, it's, I've not been known to moan.

The sheilas all seemed short to me, not one could meet my eye,
And if they looked my way at all, they'd be staring at my fly,
Which is really disconcerting, when you're young, unsure, naive,
Caught in hormonal, "no man's land" with your heart out on your sleeve.
Then my built-in suaveness left me, I'd mutter and I'd mumble,
But if there's one good thing about me, it's, I say no, to grumble.

Times of turbulence and trauma, times of doubt and times of strife,
Though I swore "it wasn't me, sir," I'm a father with a wife.
Great big wedding, guard of honour; well a shotgun, by his side,
And she had eleven brothers; there was no place left to hide.
"Wasn't yours," she told me, later, I'd been stitched up rather neat,
But if there's one good thing about me, it's, I never ever bleat.

Down the years we raised five daughters, lucky none looked much like me,
Three were nurses, one drove hearses; one was in the infantry.
Now they're all grown up and married, all got young'uns of their own,
That they love, and they're not selfish, leave 'em with, just on loan.
Interrupt my peace and quiet, it's a riot, round the clock,
But if there's one good thing about me, it's, I never does me block.

I am sure we all should, now and then, just pause and contemplate
On how others may perceive us, he's a mongrel, jeez he's great.
I have listed here, six good points, I possess, these, but a few.
As for those who claim to know me, well they wouldn't have a clue
That I'm fast approaching perfect. That'll make the family smile,
Or is it just the fact that I am maybe in denial.

Henry's Passing

There's a look you get when dying, startled headlights on a deer,
And that's the look old Henry had. Oh, he knew the end was near.
Family gathered round his bedside, vultures waiting for the end,
Only Naïve Nev his night nurse, Henry figured was his friend.
Henry's hour was fast approaching, time to leave this mortal coil,
With the wisdom born of Rhinehart, he would allocate the spoil.

"Wife, I leave to you all Pitt Street, Eldest Son, you get The Cross;
Michael, Mossman, most of Manly, toss in Bondi; that's no loss.
Sisters, Sophie and Sofia, divvy up the CBD.
My Mercedes goes to Neville, for the kindness he's shown me."
Barely had these words been spoken, when his eyes closed with a sigh,
For all ties to Earth now broken, Henry's time had come to die.

Well Nurse Neville was astounded, at what he had seen and heard.
That one man in just one lifetime, could acquire so much. "My word,"
He said, "This man, your Husband, Father, of him you must be proud,
So much property he leaves you." Wife said, "For crying out aloud,
He was useless and a skinflint, for us didn't give two hoots,
All's left's a clapped-out car, no money, and his bloody paper routes!"

My Heart Is Tranquil Now

I was seldom in a City, so to use a lift was rare.
After what occurred a while back, from now on I'll stick to stairs.
I was thinking about nothing, for which skill I am renowned,
Elevator, fast descending from the 24th to Ground,
Stops on 13, wasn't lucky, doors slide open, she steps in,
Her name tag says she's Cynthia, her lusty bust, says Sin.

I'm besotted, she's culotted, funny trouser looking things,
And her blouse clings, it arouses, and her fingers wear no rings.
I am gaping, breath escaping, could I speak it would be DER.
I am scheming, praying, dreaming, how to spend my life with her.
Then she asked me, can't believe it, "Could you press one for me, please?"
Could I press one, I caress one, gave the other one a squeeze.

Dropped her parcels, yelled, you are something, kneed me right between the legs,
Which then folded like a jack knife, swelled me bearded eggs like kegs,
I am down, not yet unconscious, that's the state I'm longing for,
Her stilletos, play staccato, pin my privates to the floor,
Doors now open, Help, I'm hoping. She yells, "pervert from the sticks."
All front rowers, all real goers, raining punches, stomping, kicks.

I awaken, hurt, forsaken, all is white, just like my cast,
It's full body, I am noddy, spot a nurse who's walking past,
Not nuh bruddy 'ell jus' happen? broken jaw, I cannot speak,
That's the caper pen and paper, find the answers that I seek.
It was gory the full story, bits and pieces I recall,
She came to visit. Feeling guilty? No, saw humour in it all.

We then dated, married, mated, live out where the lifts are rare.
Should we strike a town with high rise, we just laugh and take the stair.

The following poem is a tribute to the memory of Squadron Leader Wright and Sergeant Chandler of the RAF, who were posted to Strathpine after surviving the Battle of Britain over the English Channel. They tragically lost their lives in a midair collision on a training exercise over Sideling Creek near Petrie Queensland on the 19th of April 1944.

One April Day

The erks jump down from strapping in, they signal, "chocks away,"
The Merlins roar, dust devils dance, Spitties roll to seize the day.
The wind is gentle, Sou Sou East, climbing out, toward the sun,
Peaceful haven here, Pine Rivers, just another training run.

Here no dog-eat-dog of combat, 'neath war torn Europe's skies,
Off to port the warm Bay shimmers, off to starboard, green hills rise,
Were they bitter they'd been posted, to this backblock bushland 'drome,
Felt their talents here, were wasted, they were needed more, at home?

Did they revel in their fortune, time to live and catch their breath,
Welcome respite from the slaughter, new pals made, soon lost, to death?
Or as young men ever have been, or at least pretend to be,
"I'm six-foot-tall and bullet proof, death's for others mate, not me".

So they came and lost their lives, sudden, now devoid of cares,
In defence of our great country, same as our boys did for theirs,
Gathered here, this April morning, mourning those who gave their all,
To protect us, I believe that it behoves us to recall,
What they died for, Home and Family, the true Brotherhood of Men,
Remain vigilant and wary, for this threat will come, again.

This is normally performed, no, bad choice of words, usually is better, wearing a powder blue leotard with two big potatoes in the crutch. If I don't use them I look a trifle inadequate, in that department. I wrote this poem to make all Australians alert to the danger lurking within our midst. Saddam, Saddam Hussein. Adolph, Adolph Hitler, Idi Idi Amin were all murderers who brought misery to millions. Within our society today there hides a similar predator, Gym . . . Gymnasium, a home-grown Greek terrorist, kill you quick as look at you, do not be alarmed. Here's how I found out. I called it

Don't Ever Mention His Name

On the day that I turned seventy, my daughters, signed me up,
At the local Fitness Centre, joy, don't overflow my cup.
Now by nature I'm suspicious, questions formed inside my head,
Why? To fend off feral Grandkids, they want me prematurely dead.

But when introduced to Ingrid, lovely lithe and Lycra clad,
My own ripply, nipply trainer, I forgot those thoughts I'd had,
She looked Nordic, nubile, near nude, me I'm putty in her hands.
God she's pretty, what a pity, all I've left's, saliva glands.

As she read me her assessment, I was shocked, I thought I'd starred,
"Der few muscles, I am findink, soft, yust your arteries, they're hard",
"But no matter, ve have methods, ve vill make you big and strong,"
Fancy thinking she was Swedish, did I ever get that wrong?

For she's surely Arnold's sister, that big warts and ogre bloke.
Will she be my terminator; has this gone beyond a joke?
Whacks me on the weights, then measures, "Mein Gott," she says, "so lean,
From the many months I'm trainink, you're the veakest man I've seen."

Bugger this, I thought, who needs it, I can cop this lot at home,
So I staggers to the exit, to escape her torture dome.
"Is verboten," shrieks Miss G-string, "you must haf your money's verth,
For I see in you a challenge, the unfittest man on earth."

"Dis machine, you vill be rowink," so I tried, it somehow sank,
And I think if she'd have found one she'd have made me walk the plank.
Then that treadmill, tripping stumbling, the faster that I strode,
Why the hell did they invent this, what's the matter with a road?

Everything I've got's aquiver, cept for three bits I suspect,
Them's me kidneys, heart and liver, wrecked by long years of neglect.
"Und now we vill try the Nautilus." Is it true what I just heard?
I am not sure what a lus is, but I've heard that other word.
Struth she must be bloody kidding, not with me not in this state,
Once I could have done her bidding, but by now it's far too late.

Then she goes crook, seems my screams of pain upset her other class.
I had a real good line for here, but think I'll let it pass,
Now her dumbbells have outwitted me, I've dropped one broke me toe,
And I've started using swear words I don't even think I know.

Psychologically I'm shattered, my poor health, it's getting worse,
I see a sign, position vacant, horizontal in a hearse.
All my lustful thoughts a scratching, well in hindsight, just an itch,
No one could love this Hun from Hell, cruel anorexic bitch.

No I'll keep my sloth-like habits, and steer clear of all that's new,
Them kids'll hear, for years to come, the pain they've put me through.
Though, I'm in no shape to threaten, my prognosis, bloody grim,
I'll try to slaughter, hang and draw and quarter, anyone who mentions, Him.

Can't Win

Me, I'm drivin' slowly, surly, 'cause we've had another row,
When we passed this little paddock that contained a pig and cow.
I guess the Devil made me ask. I said, "Relatives of yours?"
She didn't bat a bloody eyelid, just said, "Yeah, they're both in-laws!"

One thing you can't compromise on is death. If you're not here you can't fix things. Give yourself some slack, being here for someone is what counts.

Feet of Clay

Role models, aren't they hard to find, someone who's kind and true,
Or does someone, strong and silent have more appeal to you?
No matter what your preference, I think it's fair to say,
That everyone I looked up to, revealed they'd feet of clay.

But did that depress me? never; it just served, to advance
My theory, that while you're alive, you get another chance
To prove yourself, so have a go, and with luck, some kid might say,
"You've taught me everything I know, and I love you, Feet of Clay.

Oh, I went through all them phases, cheating, lying, gambling, beer,
But don't tell me that's what life's about, the reason we are here.
No, what I'm trying to tell you, and not coping all that well,
Is that life does have its highs and lows, its heaven and its hell.

But while ever you are breathing, then you get another chance,
To see your Grandkids born and grow, and laugh and sing and dance.
So hang in there, mate, like I did, and who knows, maybe they'll say,
"You've taught us everything we know, and we love you, Feet of Clay."

Who Can We Trust?

You're a skeptic and a cynic, book yourself into this clinic,
And purge your paranoia, my psychiatrist said to me.
Now John, don't you get defensive, sure I know it seems expensive,
But the treatment that you'll get there's guaranteed to set you free
From your fears of persecution, mate, this place is the solution,
Bound to rid you of your distrust, put some balance in your life.
What! Who owns it? Does it matter? God I'm sick of all your chatter,
Yes Henrietta, sure, you've met her. Well, so what if she's my wife?

Misunderstood Man

From my youth I'm a frantic romantic. To excel at lovemaking my mission,
So I whispered, "Cherie, how good it would be if tonight we could change our position."
"No worries," she smiled, "Jees, you drive me wild, you voyager in affairs of the heart,
I'm a slave to your wishes so you do the dishes and I sleep in your armchair and fart!"

A Positive Attitude

A Bush Poet has been Knighted! Though not in the usual way,
Wasn't summoned to the palace, no, I made it on the day.

My Doc christened me: Sir Hosis, claimed my liver's almost shot,
Sez both lungs are bung from smoking so my future's not crash hot,
Sez my ticker's going quicker, than a ticker oughta go.
As for what's wrong with my kidneys, well nobody seems to know.

The Gastro report's scathing, on the status of my spleen,
Only six words were highlighted, "It's the worst we've ever seen."
Well at least my vision's splendid, every letter learnt by heart,
Now I've lost me Driver's Licence, sneaky new nurse, changed the chart.

Doc sez, "plumbing's problematic, leaks and blockages abound,
Don't heed the need to try and breed, cos all your swimmers drowned."
Sez, "your lifestyle's slowly killing you, I find it strange you do not worry."
"Doc," I sez, "If Slowly Killing's your prognosis, great, cos I'm not in any hurry."

Here's a little one . . .

Risk Assessment

We've ACCC on oil pricing so everything there's fine.
We've got APRA for insurance; they kept HIH in line.
We've got CASA for air safety, and the question that this begs:
Should I sack that big goanna I've got guarding my chook eggs?

Family Trilogy

This trilogy, (sounds classy don't it), was written in the early seventies when our girls were only young and so were we. If I had to pin a name on it I'd call it my pre cynicism period. That really broke Glennie, the missus, up, said when weren't you ever a cynic. Must be a perception thing.

My Family

My family would be average, if measured on a scale,
Yet I feel that we're succeeding, where so many seem to fail.
It so often seems that someone else, has got a better deal
But by chasing dreams of fancy, we can sometimes lose what's real.

I must make the time for sharing, I must take the time to care
For you. It must be hard to love someone who isn't there,
So let's work at it, not rushing, for the good things slowly grow,
While the bonds we know as family are weaving to and fro.

Giving guidance where it's needed, letting go when it seems right,
Giving strength to ward off darkness, giving laughter for the light.
Yes, I'm sure we would rate average, but that suits me just fine.
For of all the families in the world, I'm so glad that you're mine.

This next poem came about as the result of a wonderful holiday on the Hawkesbury River in 1976 and strangely enough poetically predicted what are facts today. One daughter lives with her family far away from Brisbane in Batemans Bay.

Family Ties

Far from the thrust and parry of a workday's endless grind
Comes a picture tucked forever in a corner of my mind,
Of a houseboat on still waters, a May moon on the rise,
Through misted windows watching, two young girls with wondrous eyes.
Happy times of love and laughter, sun-filled days and balmy nights,
Oh! the magic of those moments captured all of life's delights.

The years have since flown swiftly by, the teenage dramas gone,
They've both worn long white wedding gowns and from our home moved on.
We're very close though they're far away with children of their own,
Most Christmases we see them, there's the letters and the phone.
Evermore I shall remember, scenes which forged our family's ties,
Through misted windows watching, two young girls with wondrous eyes.

Last of this trilogy but not least is a reflection on Christmas day which can be a wonderful time for some and depressing for others, the main thing I think is to remember what it was originally all about.

Christmas Keeps Our Family Strong

I thank you Father of the Son whose birthday now is here,
On behalf of everyone in this family I hold dear.
Family ties can often fray if too long left neglected
So every Christmas, come what may, some where we have collected.
Not everybody can be here, Dame Fortune thrusts apart,
But those who aren't in body near are with us in their heart.

From Grandson wearing out his bike, and going like a winner,
To Granddad, dozing statesman like, an aftermath of dinner.
We've spanned the generation gap, and started life anew,
Each branch can feel the rising sap, from which this family grew.
Don't get me wrong, we've had our fights, it's not all froth and bubble,
For should they feel within their rights they don't retreat from trouble.

But twelve months cools off anyone, especially those held dear.
Please bless us Father of the Son whose birthday now is here.

I thought at seventy-two, I would be more worldly than I am. See it never occurred to me that men would, apart from operations and beards, want to have hair removed. No that's not strictly true, I knew cyclists and swimmers shaved their legs. But want to shed the lot, come on, and it's been given a name!!! Here's how I found out.

The Butch Truckerman

G'Day, I'm John, from back of Springsure, come to town, to pick up stuff,
Not there yet, big shopping centre, need some caffeine, out of puff,
Just on opening, lotsa parking, bitty car bays, all in rows,
Hope to hell they don't get busy, truck's on twenty-four of those.

Through the door, I read Brazilian, though I might sound like a dill,
If there's one thing that I do know, they're big on coffee in Brazil.
No one there, but chairs and tables, so I grab one, sit on down,
And what happened next, I tell you, they won't see me back in town.

"Why Hi, I'm Wayne, your waxer, and Golleee, aren't you hirsute?"
"Scuse me," I sez, "Her what's that?" He sez, "You're hairy and you're cute."
I sez, "You can knock off all that bulldust, I want coffee fair enough?"
"Ooh so dominant," winced The Waxer. "I just love a bit of rough, rough."

When he brings me back me coffee, struth me jaw near hits the dirt,
He's wearing, hiding nothing leather shorts, and a kinda see through shirt,
And his skin, shone, smooth and silken, from his shaven head to toes,
Like some great big newborn baby, with one black hair up his nose.

He sits down real close beside me, I'd retreat and he'd advance.
If he thinks what I think he's thinking, well he hasn't got a chance.
He leans forward, sniffs, "That's diesel, oh you drive a truck how nice,
We do deals for other truckers, let's negotiate a price."

Negotiate a price, I thought, what for, coffee in a mug?
Then he closes in on me again, oh Strewth mate, not a hug.
But he lightly touched my pocket, "That's a bulldog you've a Mack,
I have seven clients who drive those, all back and sac and crack."

What's back and sac and crack, I shout, what are you on about?
But I guess I must have scared him, he gets teary, starts to pout.
Then he sort of semi whispered, so I didn't catch the lot,
About follicles and, defoliants, and some other tommy rot.

But by now the caffeine kicked in, which is all I'd come here for,
Throw some cash down, grabbed a brochure and skedaddled out the door.
Hit the big smoke, picked me load up, heading home Wayne's on my mind.
What the hell is it they do there? I reads the flyer, and I find

That they're not just shaving sheilas' legs and you know what's, arm pits.
This Metro Mob's now on the job, true, they're tackling blokey bits.
They de-hair yer, don't that scare yer? Never knew that, geez I'm dumb.
They'll defollicle yer bollicles, tear the hair out round yer bum.

They claim that this is painless, that this is the way to look,
Where Nature stuck it they will pluck it, leave yer looking like some chook.
As for Wayne, I remain, wary, is he educator; perve?
Though I'm still dumb and hairy, I am on this learning curve,

Steep, all down to Wayne the Waxer in his little leather shorts,
And his back and sac and crack sir, for our world she takes all sorts.
But I sometimes wonder, at Wayne's wisdom, when I'm trucking hot, you know,
That you could be in deep trouble, when the stubble starts to grow.

This is a factual account of an incident that occurred to me in my late teens, and altered the direction my life took from that day forward. Only the locations have been changed to protect the townsfolk from the notoriety that descended on the good citizens of Lourdes in France. I called it:

Horse Sense

Far out beyond the Great Divide, lay another world to me,
Son of suburbia that I am, from a city by the sea.
My academic achievements were greatly admired on the coast,
But way out there, I must declare, it's horse sense that counts the most.
Oh, I'd travelled West, with youthful zest, in search of the Great Outback,
When the ute tossed it in outa Quilpie, along the Windorah track.

In the old girl's sparse shade, I ponder, what could be possibly wrong?
And try as I might, what I do is not right, and nobody comes along.
Five long hours creep slowly by, can the heat be affecting my brain?
For I swear I can hear someone talking; there, I can hear it again.
I'm standing now, and I'm looking, but the only creature I see
Is an old grey horse across the road, and he's staring straight at me.

He sorta grins and then he begins to talk in a voice quite low,
"It appears to me that your carby's blocked, clean it out and yer ute'll go."
I stand amazed, and somewhat dazed as he saunters off out of sight,
I've no other recourse but have faith in the horse and hope I can put it right,
I did as he said, God Bless him, she started first turn of the key.
I'm off down the track with no looking back, a miracle's happened to me.

Windorah's first pub, finds me braking, my God what a story I bear,
Like shot from a gun, up the front steps I run, the bar's empty, there's nobody there.
Only the barman is present, bored, polishing glasses away.
Thinks I, just you wait the tale I relate will certainly liven your day.
He poured and polished. I ranted. Never into my story, he broke,
Struth, you could have knocked me down, with a feather, when finally spoke.

"My word," he said, "You struck the grey, you should count your lucky stars,
The bay was out there last week, he knows bugger all about cars."

Should I Have Rescued This Dog?

My old dog's deaf, can hardly see,
His plumbing's shot, sits down to pee.
The wife insists, he's much like me,
Our days are nearly over.

We're both unwell, he's worse, poor pet,
With Doctors cheaper than a Vet,
If one must go, it's him, and yet,
The wife sez, "I'll keep Rover."

Cash from my Will, they operate,
They fixed him up, he's looking great,
I've barely cooled, since my cremate,
Condolences they're sending.

They come to visit, at the wall,
My plaque's down low, it's cheap and small,
He cocks his leg, I cop it all,
A far from Happy Ending.

Assassins

Is now the time to rethink Family Planning?
You don't see this as a problem, mostly past the age to breed?
But I'm talking retrospective, So, let's fertilise that seed!
There will no doubt dwell among you, Rellies, Off-spring you can't stand,
Ones you've visualised departed? I've the group to lend a hand.

Yes, I've launched The Mass Assassins, though not bound to any church,
Simply single out your sinners, we'll remove them from their perch.
We have method and commitment, we have poisoned, shot and hung,
We have stabbed and jabbed and strangled, we have smothered old and young.

Family Ties? Great for garrotting, take 'em out both far and close,
If your family tree is rotting, may suggest an overdose.
Whoa! some of us are getting nervous, I'm now checking windows, doors,
Anyone of us a target, should they scrutinise our flaws.
Cos' Mass Assassin's, just a concept, that appeared one sleepless night,
Better stop now, case some Pollie, might propose a Plebiscite.

Holdsworthy is a military prison. You'll need to know that. It's become fashionable to blame one's shortcomings and personal failures on somebody or something else. Usually an unhappy childhood. Well, I can go along with kids doing it. Gees, I was guilty of that myself. "Why can't I have a new bike?" and "How come we haven't got a car?" and "Why do we live in a housing commission?" But, when we become adults, we should realise we become responsible for our own happiness. An unhappy childhood needn't be a life sentence. Life's too short. Get over it and get on with it. I've written this poem for all those Mums who did what they had to do to make sure their kids got a good start in life. I've called it:

I'm a Lucky Son of Me Mum

My late dear Mum was no Einstein but through tough times she learned what was what.
She taught me to count all me blessings, to be happy with what was my lot.
Now some never can seem to grasp this, they always want more than they need.
Mum said, "Son, nothin' wrong with ambition – just make sure it don't turn into greed."

So I stand here before you this morning to recount wond'rous days of my youth,
A time filled with gladness – I never knew sadness. That's the God's honest truth.
Was I favoured by fate's fickle finger when I flung me hat in the ring?
Yes. Destiny picked me as special and showed what good karma can bring.

"You were born premature-which was lucky," so me spinster Aunt Ethel once said,
With sly look in her eye, "most convenient-just the bare six months after they wed."
At me birth Mum asked Daddy to name me saying "Now you make sure that it fits."
Dear old Dad with his own quirky humour said, "Why don't I just call it quits?"

As a kid people said I was ugly, though nobody says that today!
Why if Mum put me out in the sandpit, the cat covered me up straight away!
She started to call Dad "The Phantom" – he'd be here and then he'd be gone.
He grew rich selling army equipment, bad timing when the war was still on.

I asked what Dad did in the army, she said "Sonny, you don't want to hear."
But I did. Seems two years in Holdsworthy for advancin' too fast to the rear.
They gave him dishonourable discharge, then wrote on his papers "Perhaps
If you wish to assist our war effort, then re-enlist quick – with the Japs."

Now I didn't see much of him when he got out, though he'd sometimes visit me mother,
But she'd only say, "Daddy dropped in today. He was after a bit of the other."
But we never went short of family support in that period after the war.
I never met too many aunties, but I sure had them uncles galore!

Uncle Ron I remember quite fondly. He was always laughin' and jokin'.
He'd hang out in bars and had lots of cars that all had the one window broken!
I think he wound up in the police force which seemed fun and a pretty good lurk.
With the siren full on they'd pick up Uncle Ron and apparently drive him to work!

I knew I was different from other boys when I first made the kindy scene.
See they all seemed quite short and quite chubby, but then again, I was thirteen!
Later we got some new neighbours. Gees their daughter, right off the top shelf.
"Me doctor, you nursey" I'd whisper. She'd bellow "Go play with yourself!"

Now me Granny said, "This is unhealthy, hormonal, you'll find it soon passes."
But how would she know? She was young long ago and besides, I don't even need glasses!
Voluptuous best describes me first love. She had four lovely cheeks-all with dimples.
I'd beg her to stray. She'd say, "Put that away. If I squeeze anything it's your pimples!"

I remember sweaty nights at the pictures. All in wrestlin' , those big canvas seats
Never ever got to the finals, but we got pretty hot through the heats.
I can see some of ya out there comparin' was my childhood better or worse?
Though light on for cash I was heavy on flash, see I bought me a second-hand hearse.

I'll stop soon for I sense some are stroppy 'cause I've trod such a fortunate track.
In me shiny black wagon-great for drinkin' 'n' faggin' I knew I was truly laid back.
Me Dad, he took off like they used ta. He went out for a packet of smokes
And never came back. Me Mum, never dumb, grabbed one of the other blokes.
She got a divorce and remarried, oh pick of the crop he was too,
Honest and carin' he loved all of us, bit worse for the war but true blue.

I'd love to return if you'll have me. Sometime in the future, no doubt,
And tell you the rest of this story, what became of that laidback young lout.
See you can't pick your rellies or parents. Nah, it's only your friends you can choose,
And I hope and I pray with what we've shared here today that I've made some new friends amongst youse.

Contemporary Bush Poetry reflects Australia's life today and historically has provided a powerful vehicle for social change. Maybe not this poem, but who knows? I wrote this in 2002 and now we have a national inquiry. I've called it:

Are the Elderly Revolting?

I have reached the autumn of my life, which wasn't that flash, in its summer.
That's me, you see I have always marched to the beat of another drummer.
But I like to think I can end my days and round this great land roam,
For I've a dread of the living dead locked up in a bad nursing home.

To the aged it's a sensitive issue, to the young just a smile, maybe shrug
But I know you seldom find answers to problems swept under the rug.
So if laughter be the medicine, let's tackle this with humour.
What's he on about? Let me spell it out and dispense with the myth and rumour.

Those caring honest operators – this is not about you, I should stress.
It's those few, the heartless and greedy, who attract all the unwanted press.
Yes, you've a problem Canberra and my thoughts on the problem I'll share.
There's a need to review the one you have who is responsible for aged care.

For a start there's the problem of image which should be addressed with vigor.
Who can reconcile that aggressive style with a caring mother figure?
I've no doubt she's a very nice person but on TV she makes me go tense.
She purses her lips, seems to shoot from both hips. She'd be far better off in defence!

From defence, it's not far to travel back to, dare I mention, a war?
When the Poms built a camp concentration, you know in that blue with the Boer.
From there it's only a hop step and jump if you leave your thoughts free to roam
And what do you get? Your worst nightmare yet – you guessed it, a bad nursing home

In some homes you'll find shelter and comfort and their owners should all be applauded.
Yet others deserve to be closed down, for they're not what the doctor ordered.
Or are they? Who owns all these places? Whose is the money invested?
Do their interests conflict? Some may, I predict, and this certainly needs to be tested.

Now I've spoken at length to these seniors. I do poetry for them, then chat
And slowly I've reached a conclusion–there's other places they'd rather be at.
There's a groundswell of disenchantment, now a whisper-it'll soon be a shout
It's not good enough. They're doin' it tough. I can picture a mass breakout.

See I've checked out their library records and these lines you should all read between –
Three most popular books? "The Great Escape", "Papillon" and "Stalag 17".
The local TAFE's not unsympathetic: anti-nursing home protests they've staged
To show that they care they've sewn bags for hot air and taught tunnelling to the aged.

So, don't be surprised if one morning balloon squadrons float over your fence.
There'll be no spring chickens in these baskets and the hot air? Yeah, flatulence.
And don't ring the law, please just ignore those depressions in your front lawn
It's a tunneller, mate. When he reaches your gate by tomorra, he'll be gone

Should they not have the strength to leave on their own, this issue I will not shirk.
They'll just laptop their mate in a wheelchair. Please note here the genius at work,
Vision impairment? No problem! I've a scheme I admit I've not tried,
See, I'm breedin' these bloody big guide dogs. They'll just hop in the saddle and ride!

And you mob, if drivin' near nursin' 'omes spot someone a little bit older,
They're not hard to pick – they've a walker or stick with a furtive look over their shoulder.
Do the right thing! Lend 'em a hand, render whatever assistance.
Your turn'll come 'round, now known underground "Paid up member of Senior Resistance."

As you've gathered by now, I'm across this. Those that can flee will have flown.
I've no doubt solved most of their problems and those left behind, "Home Alone".
Yes Minister, you've done some good work. Give credit where credit is due,
But I think, and I'm not alone thinkin', that we should do better. Don't you?

For these folk and their like forged this nation, this country of which we're so proud.
Some gave up their youth for Australia, others gave up their lives, brave, unbowed.
Minister, is this how we repay them? For this did they work, fight and die?
We can and we must do this better, or is "Lest We Forget" now a lie?

You'll either get this poem or you won't. Good Luck.

Robbie Rabbit

This is a true tale of Robbie, a laboratory rabbit from birth.
Above shone bright neons, instead of the stars while below, stainless steel, 'stead of earth.
But one rabbit's foot can bring you good fortune and of course lucky Robbie had four.
When Opportunity knocked and the building unlocked, that rabbit just hopped out the door.
Oh how sweet was the feel of the grass 'neath his feet as he wide-eyed beheld his first Dawn.
He knew then the feeling of freedom and that this then was why he was born.

Past the hedges he saw, others like him, he couldn't believe his good luck,
When he hopped through, he knew he belonged with this crew, their leader said "G'day I'm Buck."
"G'day mate I'm Robbie ex lab/rab and this my first day on the loose.
I haven't a clue what you wild rabbits do, in fact I feel more like a goose."
"No worries" said Buck. "We can train you if you watch what we do then you'll know.
See these carrots we eat, they're so juicy and sweet, bound to increase your get up and go."

Well they cropped and they hopped and they bloody near dropped and Robbie had not known such fun,
There was cabbage and spinach and lettuce and eventually his first setting sun.
Oh it's magical cried out our Robbie what else can you wild rabbits do?
"What else," said old Buck, "Well we could try our luck with the girls", and Rob's interest grew.
So we'd best now suppose that Rob knows about Does as would any red-blooded rabbit.
No they don't need no learning when they get the yearning, research shows it's a natural habit.

"Yes those Does were fantastic," Rob reckoned. "The best day of my life I have spent."
And he queried if there were more carrots, claiming his get up and go had just went.
Buck, "Why don't you come live in our warren, we all think that you're our sort of bloke."
"No, though I think freedom's fab, I must return to the lab, 'cause I'm just dying for a smoke."

Certain events in life may prompt one to pause and reflect what it's all about. Where do I go from here? These events can include the death of a friend or a loved one, a personal near-death experience, birthdays ending in zero or the birth of your first grandchild as it was in my case. These are major events and many people may reflect more frequently for other reasons. However, I think it is important that we step back now and then and do this, and see the options available. We are, throughout our lives, coming to forks in the road and having to make decisions: do we want to live in a society as a people, or in an economy as a unit of work? Or is the latter the only option, given the money and consequently the power, is in so few hands? I hope not. I've called this:

On Our Election

You'll get a chance one Saturday to turn our country 'round,
Scrub this me-me-me economy, get back to safer ground.
For people make a country great and how we treat each other.
Worship other gods than money? You'd better believe it, brother.
Why spare me days it's user pays that's what some now see as fair.
Then what about all those without who find their cupboards bare?
Desert them in their hour of need and toss 'em on a heap?
Is life only for the rich and strong? In graveyards where they sleep,

Great Australians past are turning and twisting in their tombs.
Fred Hollows, Weary Dunlop, Sister Kenny, Nugget Coombs.
Why were these people so revered and held in in such esteem?
Was it 'cause they'd lots of money? No, these people had a dream
That they could make things better for all those who had much less
In health and social standing. As Australians we should bless
The very ground they walked on and those thousands less well-known
Who through attitude and action and the way they lived had shown

They truly cared for other people. Now Australians can begin
To care for one another so let's back the human race to win.

This poem was written in 1998 for Steve Bredhauer when he became the Minister for Transport in Queensland. I retired a couple of weeks later albeit from the opposite end of the corporate ladder, and I offered this poem as advice. The term "Better Transport for Queensland" is the Department's Mission Statement, CV is Curriculum Vitae, DG is Director General, the Minister's 2IC and QT stands for Queensland Transport. Though written with Queensland Transport in mind, I believe it holds true for most large corporations.

The Good Drum
Steve, you've got a right lot here, not that I know them all
You've anarchists and dinosaurs and some too strange to call
You've plodders who will do you proud whose songs will go unsung
And others I call butterflies who flit from rung to rung
Upward, ever upward, on the strength of their CV
Who are flashy on the surface, but a danger to QT
For underneath there's little that's of value to this group
And if you let them fly too high they'll land you in the soup

So when you go recruiting for advisors as you must
Look beyond their resumes. Look for people you can trust
Who'll tell you you're a dickhead should you tread a track that's wrong
Rid yourself of sycophants, all those who'll go along
With anything the boss says, "Oh, Yes Minister. You're right"
Surround yourself with people who will scratch and claw and fight
To make sure you get the picture as it is, not how it seems
Then Better Transport for Queensland will be real, not just a dream

You're a lucky man, Steve Bredhauer for you've landed on your feet
You've drawn a great Department, a DG who's hard to beat
Bruce Wilson's tried and tested, a good listener and he hears
The pulse that beats within your charge so let him be your ears
And eyes and you must trust that he'll not let you come unstuck
But Steve and Bruce, with due respect, you'll also need some luck
To dodge the many pitfalls that a folio of this size
Presents on a daily basis and so I humbly advise

That you'll have to make your own luck if you're going to succeed
So I offer now this recipe I think you're going to need:
Take a handful of honest people across the range of age
The young will give you vibrancy, the old a hint of sage
You mix 'em in and stir them up and add a bit of time
People people, Steve and Bruce, I think you'll find that I'm
Giving you the good drum, you the folk to lead this band
To make your Queensland Transport the finest in the land.

The Calathumpian Religion believes in re-incarnation, I am aware that this is a little-known fact as I have just made it up. We'll go from there . . .

Devious Devils

What devious devils you dames are, who I once thought were simply naive,
You all have your secret agendas, while we blokes wear our heart on our sleeve.
Mine, signed me up as a Calathumpian, great I thought, she wants more of the same,
But no; this was not her intention, far too late I woke up to her game.

That Big Copper up there in Heaven, must have thought I failed some sort of test,
Couldn't have been cleaner, I saw no subpoena, he just nailed me with cardiac arrest.
A night on a slab, but not one you'd grab from the pub, if you've drinking in mind,
A pretty cool place, I've a smile on my face, for I've left all my troubles behind.

Soon I'm rushed off to Gow's, aren't they nosy cows? poking around in my bits,
Cheap pinewood box, dressed me up, socks and jocks, shirt and tie, the old suit, struth it fits!
They all mills around, with sadness profound, but I detect some aren't actually grieving,
Oh but they will, when I give them a thrill, see I'm lying here, still, shallow breathing.

Well they wheel me on into the Chapel, one castor could use some more oil,
Funny what you think in a coffin, but a squeaking wheel makes my blood boil.
Open of course, with my knees up, makes me wonder just what they had planned.
Would I arrive knock-kneed or bandy, should I get to the Promised Land?

The Rev's revving them up, earning his money, weighing up my goodness and sin,
I can tell you, he, very near snuffed it, when I leapt to my feet with a grin.
" There'll be none of this dearly departed, you're getting off on the wrong track,
I'm a born again Calathumpian, and I'm here to tell you, that I'm back!"

This then, was my moment of glory, when my missus yelled something that smarted,
She cried, " Bloody good, you can buy some more wood, and finish those jobs, that you've started!"

It's obvious that not everyone can be a shearer or a drover. There are other things that people can do to keep this country going. No matter what, if it's Australian, it has a place in our poetry of our past and future. Let me introduce you to an old mate of mine who, though he's passed on, remains fondly in my memory. "Scrambled eggs" is the gold braid that senior officers wear on their caps. I've called this one:

Forget Mondays

In the sixties, Barney was the barber, at the RAAF Base Williamtown,
And his only style, was shear the lot, from the ear'oles, straight on down.
He was known to like a natter, as shin-deep in hair he'd toil,
And I'd often drop into his shop, when seeking the "Good Oil".
As a barber he was ord'nry, or perhaps that's being kind,
But as a source of worldly wisdom, no one better springs to mind.

As a bloke he was a bottler; full of life and full of wit,
Except maybe for Mondays, when he'd front up, none too fit.
For he was a "Social Bowler", spent weekends, well, near the green,
And those in the know, said, "Don't you go to Barney – on Mondays, I mean."
He suffered from "Post Bowling Tension", though the face he'd put on, was quite brave.
On Mondays I felt, by his look, how he smelt, there'd be healthier men in the grave.

It was painful, to sit there and watch him, he'd arrive, take the phone off the hook,
I'd talk the most, Barn as white as a ghost, if he spoke, just said, "Jesus, I'm crook."
"Well why not go home?" I suggested, "take some Aspros and climb on the bed?"
"What and let on to 'er, that I'm suffrin'. Son I'd be better off, bloody dead."
But the other four days, he was special, and four outa five's not too bad,
Like a Faraway Father for some of us, and for others, the Dad they'd not had.

See, he'd ponder your personal problems, then he'd say, "I'm not sure, but I think . . . "
And I'm still in awe of the things that I saw, yeh, he saved more than one, from the brink.
He was sort of part Padre, part Prophet, but not in the God-bothering mould,
When I mentioned it once, he said "Don't be a dunce, it'll come to you son, when you're old."
There was nothing escaped his attention, see that Base couldn't run without Barn,
Or someone like him, though their chance'd be slim, and old Barney could tell a good yarn.

This one, well he swore it was gospel, stack of bibles, said it happened right there,
And though I've oft heard it since, no one will convince me that Barney was not on the square.
Seems the CO and a Sergeant were seated, (Barney hired extra help in a rush).
Both were nearing the end of their haircuts, just the clippings from shoulders to brush,
"Bay Rum for you, Sir," asked the hired hand? " God No," said the CO, put out,
"Wife'll think that I've been in a brothel." Then he left, "Scrambled Eggs" with the gout.

"Bay Rum for you, Sarge?" asked old Barney. "Rub it in" said the Sarge, "that's the style."
"See my missus don't know what a brothel smells like." Then he turned to those there with a smile.
Looking back, growing old and remembering, those folk welcome most in my mind
Are not winners and grinners, who'd sometimes turn mean; but the battlers, the laughers, the kind.
No, Old Barney weren't much of a barber, more a teacher I s'pose, of young blokes,
And down through the years, to recall him still cheers. I salute him, the man, and his jokes.

This event really happened, only the dog's name has been altered, for no other reason than I got it wrong and by the time I found out, I had written the damn poem and wasn't about to rearrange it. So wherever Buster is mentioned, the dog's actual name was Butch. Sadly, owner Don has now passed on and his daughters requested I read this poem at his funeral.

St Don, the good butcher of Petrie

There's not a lot going down, around our town, 'cepting of course for the sun,
Few legends I've found, they're thin on the ground, 'cepting of course, for this one.
While Assisi may have their Saint Francis, and all animals call him, Patron,
The Petrie dog pack is just itching to back, for beatification, Our Don.

Our Don who, what did he ever do, is this bid for Sainthood true and sound?
Mc Neven's his name, freeing dogs is his aim, yes, he was the one, stormed the pound.
Oh he'd seen more than his fair share of trouble, for his family had just hit the toe,
His life now was grog, work and Buster his dog, but woe as you know tends to grow,

For our Donny, as so often happens when your star is beginning to wane,
Someone comes along, with their number tens on, whacks one in, then it's downhill again.
His nemesis, a devoted Dognapper, keenest worker you'll find in this Shire,
Found poor Buster astray and whisked him away, soon a prisoner behind council wire.

That Baskerville mob, could be out of a job, the way Buster was howling that night,
There was more than a score, some unloved, some adored, all sharing the same tragic plight.
Oh, there was much whining, no dining, with freedom and food, just a dream,
But, Buster's Dad Don, had his thinking cap on, and was working at home on his scheme.

See butchers have good stuff that dogs love, the top place to shop in their eyes,
And though on the grog, Donny yearned for his dog, and his IQ was starting to rise.
"I'll spring him," he thought," not a problem, grab some meat, then climb in, toss him out,
It's past mid-night and raining like buggery, there's bound to be no one about."

But his goodness then proved his undoing, his compassion would not be denied,
Not just Buster he sprung, but every poor mong, bar the guard dog, though Don claims he tried.
Came the dawn, with the keeper to feed them, vacant cages, the odd scrap of rump,
There asleep in the corner like little Jack Horner, the guard dog by now looking plump.

Well the Poundman went right off his cruet, as you would, if you'd been in charge there.
With the meat in his mit he drove off in a fit, to share all his cares with the Mayor.
Well Mayor Yvonne agreed, a dastardly deed, acts like this could catch on, if not stopped,
The Demons got busy, fitted Don. "Well who is he"? she asked, then she bloody near dropped.

"Oh! not Donny," she cried. "He's just lost his bride, this could start him downhill on the skids,
And on top of that, he pops in for a chat, and he's babysat all of my kids."
But too public, too heinous to bury, the case soon appeared in our court.
When they mentioned a sentence suspended, "Struth! Can they hang me?" Don thought.

But the Beak he was not without humour, though stern faced as all judges must be.
Don was fined, no conviction recorded, which he paid, and was shortly turned free.
The Judge then summoned our Don to approach him, and whispered, "There is one more thing.
Is it OK if I keep your number, so when they grab mine, I can give you a ring?"

Oh, there's not a lot going down, around our town, 'cepting of course for the sun,
But if a Saint ever comes, those prone to sniff bums, agree with me, Don, you should be the one!

A little something for the golfers:
Driving Hazards

From tee to green and in between in fairway, rough, and sand,
No greater advocate of golf exists in this great land
Than me but now I've done me dash. Me eyes are on the blink.
I know that's what they're s'posed to do, but mine are stuffed, I think.
It's okay when I swing it sweet and fluke one up the middle
But even then, how far it's gone has now become a riddle.
And should I play the army game, left right, left right, you see
It could be anywhere at all – bedammed or up a tree.

So, no. Bugger it. I'll sell me clubs and maybe take up bowls.
That's what them oldies seem to do 'fore they're put in their holes.
But there's figures they don't tell ya. The most dangerous game around
Is bowlin', yeah-you take it up and soon you're six foot underground!
You just check up in the obits. You'll find it's true, what I've suggested,
'Cause after RSLs it's bowls clubs whose members are requested
To attend the funeral of Tom, Dick, Harry or whoever.
No. I'll stall a while, not push me luck. It don't seem all that clever.

I'll see the pro. He's bound to know what my next step should be.
He's a know-all bastard, there's few smarter men than he
If you ask him. So I did. He reckoned that "I think your only hope
Is to try a round with Freddie who we've christened *Telescope*."
For he can see into the future though he's quite doddery and old.
I think if you team up with him you'll be as good as gold.
So I did. We teed off early as the mist began to rise.
This would normally be a worry. Not today. I've Freddie's eyes.

Well I creamed one and it felt great. Off it flew, I knew not where.
"Holy Jesus," cried old Freddie. "What a beauty! Got it there!"
Well, his dribbled 50 metres and he bounced it off a tree.
Two air swings then connection. Guess the golf God heard my plea!
Now we're a fair way up the fairway out in Shark-and-Tiger-land,
And though Fred's not feelin' all that flash, I'm feelin' pretty grand!
"Okay Fred, old mate, where is it?" I can't wait to check the length.
Then Fred seemed to age quite quickly while I muttered, "Give me strength!"

For he'd propped and looked around him in a confused worried state,
Scratched his head, then other places, then he said, "I'm sorry, mate.
Though my vision's perfect, I've this flaw, strewth I feel rotten,
I've no doubt I saw it land but, just where, seems I've forgotten!"
And so in response to past suggestion, and of them there's been a few,
Like, you find them much more easily if you use balls that's new.
Well that's okay for all you rich young blokes, who casually mention,
But old balls are what you're stuck with when you're on the old age pension.

The government stated the other day there was a critical shortage of nursing home beds. Surprise! Surprise! The article was written so cleverly that, by the end of it I was feeling quite guilty for having grown older quicker than expected, thus causing them this embarrassment. It's my firm belief that they employ more spin doctors than MDs. You take voluntary euthanasia . . . as soon as we get used to that, it'll probably become compulsory! So, in order to do my bit for the country, I wrote this piece to try and dissuade people from wanting to go into nursing homes. It's called:

Our Big Day Out

That big bus outside our Nursing Home is bright and shiny, new,
Not at all like us who'll use it, we've clocked up a klick or two.
Half of us don't want to be here, and the others; wouldn't know,
But to-day's our day for outings, and the Sister said, "You go."

Oh, she's got seven shades of sourness; no one's ever seen her smile,
But I get the funny feeling that she would, if we'd Sieg Heil.
We're formed in a semi-circle, as the bus they start to load,
We tend to spend more time like this, than we do on the road.

There's Walter in his wheelchair and Frances on her frame,
They've labeled us like luggage, I bet nobody's game to claim,
And we're heading for the Gold Coast, won't this be a jolly romp,
We, who can recall its early days, think skeeters, sandflies, swamp.

Now we're humming down that highway, singing hits from days of yore,
With long skinny Winnie whinging, "My poor bum is getting sore,"
Some Saint, who doubles as our driver, shouts, "Cheer up, we're nearly there."
"That's Bloody Bullshit," cries big Eddy. "Oops, I'm not supposed to swear.

Klepto Clare claims she's been touched up, and wants the culprit caught.
The Saint points and says, "Sit up here, my dear, I think you're overwrought."
But when mild mannered Mildred mentions that someone has groped her too
Simon Templar screeches to a halt, well what else can he do?

He's weary, walks back down the aisle, sees Fred down on his knees,
Who says, "I've dropped me bloody glasses, can you help me find them please?"
The mystery's solved, when Freddy adds, "And I've lost me new toupee,
Twice there, I felt I'd found it, but both times, it got away!"

As you've probably gathered by now, mine wasn't a classical education, but I do read a lot. Recently I read where, by the time I'm 80 I'll be outnumbered by women by six to one! This got me to thinking-what sort of a creator would give a man those odds when the equipment he most needs to best take advantage of 'em is probably well past its use by date? Conversely, I thought, as we lateral thinkers do, when you're about 14 or 15, give or take a year, when your hormones are whizzing around like crazy and your little swimmers are clockin' up sub-Olympic qualifying times, you find out-in hindsight of course-that that same creator didn't supply your body with enough blood for your brain and your other bits to work at the same time! This poem was about that moment in a young man's life, not necessarily mine. I'm in denial. It's called:

It Pays to Listen

I've never done well with the ladies, never seemed to possess what it took.
If they spoke then I'd stammer and stutter. If they touched me, well Jesus I shook
Though blessed with dress sense by St. Vincent who runs them boutiques with de Paul,
Clothes when draped from this frame all look the same as when hung from a nail in the wall.

Well, we'd all come on down from the bush into town so me Mum could be closer to Dad
Who'd scored five years work at the prison, livin' in, the longest job he'd ever had.
Me employed straight away, nightsoil carter, grade-A, for me Mum quite a pleasant surprise
She'd padded me hat an' said, "Don't trust the rust or you'll get more than smoke in your eyes."

She says funny things like that sometimes but I haven't a clue what she means.
But why should I care? Now a lair with some flair with me pink shirt and snake-proof black jeans
I'd made some new friends at this milk-bar which was where we laid-backs hung about
Seems two of their uncles broke rocks with me Dad while another had just broken out.

One kind friend said, "Difference unsettles. It's ya height that's against ya, ol' mate,
But if they can't see ya, no worries. So I'll set ya up with a blind date."
Well, it turned out he wasn't that friendly, or as kindly as he claimed to be
For the girl he lined up at the Ekka called Shirl, strewth she could see better'n me!

She didn't say much, except for, "Don't touch," as we rode on the big ferris wheel,
And as we explored sideshow alley, seemed bored, so I lashed out and bought her a meal
"And what would you like to do now?" I enquired. She replied, "I just wanna get weighed."
So into the tent of 'Guess Your Weight Man' we went and I watched as 'is hands 'round her strayed.

"Eight stone neat on the button," he quoted. So help me she said, "That's spot on!"
Then they grinned at each other like lovers while I mourned where me two bob 'ad gone.
Well, I fed her a fairy floss fortune. She pigged out on popcorn and Coke.
We whipped, roller-coastered and dodged 'em and then for the fourth time she spoke,

"I just wanna get weighed," she implored me. Strewth, I reckoned she'd gained half a stone.
But I'd had enough of this romancin' stuff. Felt I'd be better off on me own.
So we caught the tram home to her suburb. Silence makes for a very long trip.
As she walked down the hall I stuck me ear to the wall, hopin' to pick up some tip.

Her Mum said, "You're home early Shirley. You usually don't get in 'til dawn."
Shirl said, "Mum, it was wousey he just wouldn't wisten." Me? Well, I wished that I'd never been born!

Have you ever been given something that winds up costing you more than it was worth in the first place? Something that, in hindsight, you'd have been better off refusing or taking straight to the dump? Life's like that. It can drive you 'round the twist. This one's called

It's All in the Mind, I Think . . .

I can tell that some of you have suffered and like me, cry more than laugh,
Go straight to the head doctor, and don't do things by half.
Mine said, "You're a paranoid apathetic," which I figured was fair enough.
See, I knew the whole world was out to get me but I didn't give a stuff.
And here's just one example of how I wound up that way.
We'd called in at the in-laws where I heard her father say,
"We've finished our extensions, all new paint and polished floors,
And I've this surplus sliding window. You can have it son, it's yours.

No, don't even mention money, it's from us to you, a gift."
Ooh I shoulda looked in that horse's mouth. Well, didn't it cause a rift
In our marital relations. Oh we've had some since but that's when
I shoulda told him where to fit it, but I was tactful then.
Renovators dream. They do you know, I reckon that's the truth.
The wife flew off with the fairies, more like a nightmare, strewth.
She starts buyin' "House and Garden", and "Home Beautiful" and such,
When I points out we're war service and more like a rabbit hutch.

She says, "How typical! So negative! Can't think what I saw in you!"
Snidely I suggested, "Bob the builder and his crew?"
Well! That was deemed unworthy of response of any kind,
And she's awfully hard to sidetrack when she makes up her mind.
Well we can levitate it, you know, lift it up then build in underneath,
A guest room with an ensuite. "Why? We ain't got one," I said through gritted teeth.
"Perhaps a proper games room," I then heard magic fingers say,
And I thought, with all this flamin' work when would we get to play?

But I dunno why I bothered. All me protests were in vain.
You'd have thought by then a bloke woulda learned if he had half a brain.
She was obviously committed, and I thought it wouldn't hurt
To jack it up and dig it out, walk on concrete 'stead of dirt.
Well, we didn't need no budget 'cause we never had no dough,
And it's surprising what you can achieve with who, not what, you know.
So with me architectural angel there a harpin' in the wings,
Our lives took new direction. We started learnin' builder's things.

We met this mob called Wallaby Jack, Bob Cat and Accro Props.
We begged and borrowed and often acquired but never drew the cops.
See I was workin' on that theory, the means justifies the ends.
But we're still payin' back the favours 'cause I used a lot of friends.
Plans and council approvals? Oooh, not back then, you see.
Besides, if they knew what you were up to they'd bung on a building fee.
But them councils though, cunning sods, got us some years down the track
But by then banks'd lend us some money and, with luck they might get it back.

Now, about that free bloody window; just one wouldn't do of course,
Five others arrived late one evening by way of a pseudo-gift horse.
A mate of a mate's cousin in glazing aware of our need, lack of buck
Brought 'em, unbroken. Amazing! Fair drop off the back of his truck!
It became a logistical nightmare: RSJs, paint, timber, two doors,
Built-ins, a shower and toilet, tiles for the walls and the floors.
We discovered skills buried within us, unknown, lying dormant, asleep.
The angel said, "Some of yours still seem quite knotty and those buried are down bloody deep."

Well, it's that sorta support that sustained me throughout all that trouble and strife
From whence springs that wonderful cliché behind every good man's a great wife.
See they know how to press all your buttons what makes you stop, makes you go.
It's them makes important decisions you just think that you're runnin' the show.
Well, it's finished. It's paid for. It's history and we think it turned out rather grouse.
It's cool in the summer, warm in the winter, the best bloody room in the house.
Gone paranoia and apathy, gone that moper you met at the start,
Replaced by this lateral thinker, and I hope from my tale you'll take heart.

See I'm workin' full-time in psychiatry, the doc stands me in front of his class,
Then he tells them, "he thinks he's the full bloody window but he's only a pane in the glass."

I think I'm basically a serious writer who gets upset over something which prompts the start of a poem. This then deteriorates into flight of fancy. I find it hard to maintain the rage. It's far easier to pinch an old joke and adapt it to what you're on about. Hence this one:

Hello Dolly

"Ethics must keep pace with science," frightening words brought instant fear,
For they contradicted my beliefs, the values I hold dear.
Yeah, that statement near unhinged me watchin' TV half asleep,
For it was made by some professor who'd just built a bloody sheep.
Now "Hello Dolly" had new meaning, not the one I'd always known.
Ooh I knew the Scots were frugal but a cheaper sheep? A clone?
Where the hell's this gonna lead to now their foot's inside the door?
I bet this won't satisfy them; they'll be clambering for more.

Like: we've got this girl, Gorilla, so intelligent, oh she's great,
We were wondering if it's possible to find her a human mate.
Yes. The genetic gentry chuckle. Somewhere there's bound to be
Someone who'll put a whole new slant on animal husbandry.
So they drew up a list of attributes their target should possess
'Hairy' figured prominently, as did 'works well under stress'.
'Strong physique' was deemed important, 'must have stamina to burn.
'Be well spoken'? No. Why bother? Body language, he's soon learn.

If possible they'd seek a man whose hands could brush the ground,
And, probably, he'd lack a neck; all agreed that would be sound.
Then his IQ raised some questions; they agreed they preferred 'low',
So they set their sights on Sydney. Only, where else would you go?
'Devoid of morals' struck a chord; used car sales? Or a banker?
No. Their profile fitted only one – the dreaded union flanker!
But who would do? They'd not a clue just which one to approach.
So, all shifty-eyed and old-school-tied, they sought a rugby coach!

The old-boy network soon revealed a defrocked neurosurgeon.
I've just the man – 'tis Dunghead Dan – but he may need some urgin'.
Ooh urgin's what we're good at, laughed the Chairman of the Board.
Go tell your man, this Dunghead Dan, "Ten grand's all we can afford."
The ex-Nappa-Capper fronted Dan and, over the odd drink,
Explained the situation-in monosyllables I think.
Dunghead jumped at the idea. "Imagine! Me! I'll be the first.
To ever mate with a gorilla! Gees I've got a bloody thirst!"

Their glasses rose, their glasses fell, Dan's thoughts became quite muddled
And Dan's thoughts sober weren't too bright, and dimmed when booze befuddled.
Who'll believe it? Me? Old Dunghead, the most famous man on earth!
Coach, they heard you mention money, come again now, what's it worth?"

"Ten grand's the figure mentioned, son. I assume you're hot to trot?"
"No. No. I need to think on this, to work out what is what."
"Don't dally Dan. Time's money. Patience not this group's long suit,
And in keeping with your background, they just might give you the boot."
"Boot? Huh? Yeah, that's pretty funny. Meet ya here. Tomorra. Four.
I'll probably have some questions, but I'm interested for sure."
All through the night Dan racked his brain and weighed the cons and pros.
Smart people weigh 'em in reverse, but Dan weren't one of those.

They met. Said Dan, "Coach, I'm your man if these three things you'll tick . . . "
"Dan hear me boy, no greater joy, but don't bung it on too thick."
"So, this gorilla; she's a girl, right? Pretty? Yeah, okay.
Phew, that's been playin' on me mind. You've really made my day.
Now it'll probably take a keg to throw the leg. Big steps I'm taking soon.
I'll be up there with that hamstrung bloke who walked upon the moon!
So, you'll buy that? Right. Just one last thing. See, me credit's none too flash,
Do you reckon they'd give me a few more days to try and raise the cash?"

Long John Best

This next one I've had hangin' around for years. It's called:

What's Fair

By Jeez, I've had a gutful, of these people that you meet,
Who walk and talk peculiar, why are they out on the street,
Struth, some of them can't even walk; they ride in chairs on wheels.
Don't they ever stop to wonder how uncomfortable it feels
To have to look at them, and listen, to the funny sounds they make?
We've got to find a better way, for everybody's sake.

Let's build more institutions and lock 'em out of sight,
And if they must get out at all, then let 'em out at night
When I don't have to see 'em, 'cause I'm sensitive, you see.
What do you all reckon listeners, are there any more like me,
Who believe that as Australians, we deserve some Human Rights?
No don't let 'em out in daylight, just keep 'em locked up tight.

'Cause if we don't try and stop 'em now, while we've still got a show,
And they get an education; they'll get half smart you know,
And be wanting jobs, and asking why, they can't be like us?
And get around this country, in a train or plane or bus.

And then God help us, housing, and next we're off overseas
To the Para- bloody-lympics and then the whole world, Jeez'll
Know we're not all perfect, not all long and lean and tough,
I ask you fellow Aussies, is this good-e bloody nough.

No of course it's not, these issues have been hanging round for years,
But when they were raised, met eyes that glazed, or fell upon deaf ears.
Can we not see, the inequity, is it so hard to find?
Or have we perhaps, heaven forbid, selectively gone blind?

So you, yes you, your smugness, with your "I'm all right Jack" smile,
Got life by the short and curlies eh; well you listen up a while,
The disabled, migrants, oldies, you give us half a chance,
And we'll try and change this country; all we want is to advance,
Our lot in life and probably, improve yours getting there,
And so I pose this question, is to Advance-Australia Fair?

This was written prior to Iraq. I have the utmost respect for our servicemen and women. My problem is with politicians. Should this distress those who are grieving over their losses in October 2002, I sincerely apologise. This was not my intent. However, I thought this needed to be said. It's called:

Forever Overdue

How thin the thread, alive then dead, how tenuous the link
Which ties us to our loved ones, of Bali now I think.
Of children born in those far lands, who full of wonder flew,
In innocence to foreign strands, who now are overdue.
Forever overdue.

Forever young, they shall remain, in memory and heart,
No more to feel life's joy or pain, a laugh or teardrop start.
Cut down, not knowing why or how such brutal bastardry
Can change an unjust world somehow, no, that's for you and me.
Yes that's for you and me.

Revenge is sweet, the war drums beat, but we know that's not true.
Let no more sup this grief-filled cup, the way these families do.
Is this a wake-up call, perhaps? In some misguided way,
To place us in another's shoes, that they wear, day by day.
They must wear, day by day.

A call to arms is on the wind, heed not this rush of blood,
Lest that which is a trickle now, may soon become a flood.
Such thoughts we dread, sons, daughters dead, no more to grace our door.
Not those who lead, nor theirs will bleed, should we descend to war.
Do not descend to war.

Yes grieve with those whose loss is vast, and those who pain endure,
But don't rush into war too fast, for we must all ensure
That those in power, lead us not, where once our fathers trod.
So help them through their darkest hour, and listen to your God,
Yes, listen to your God.

And whatever God you listen to, I think that you will find,
Not one agrees such acts as these will bring you peace of mind.
For these are deeds of evil men, which no God can condone.
No true religion preaches hate; they've acted on their own.
These men are all alone.

Someone told me this was illusory, whatever that means it sounds pretty flash. It's called:

Verandah Dreaming

Good to see you old mate, I've missed you of late, have you been just a little bit off?
Pull up a chair, oh you've got your own there, twenty-eight inch wheels—bloody cough.
Hey remember as kids, we used to do skids on our pushies with big wheels like that?
No pneumatics of course, solids; bucked like a horse, but Jesus they never went flat.

These kids of to-day, they dunno how to play, they say Gramps put TV on, we're bored,
Then they up and they prance, like they've ants in their pants, that music's a crime to record.
So what's with this chair, you've still got your legs there, aren't you bunging it on a bit, Fred?
Them legs saved your life, when you got into strife, with that farmer, I thought you were dead!

He must have seen me, though I hid up a tree when he lined up that 12 gauge on you,
Well struth, I knew you could run, but outrun a gun, Christ mate! you bloody near flew!
Proved a decent old bloke, liked a bit of a joke, and showed that he wasn't no dobber,
Left Mum a box with a note, still remember he wrote, "melons for felons", your cobber.

Oh but we never knew, when he lined up on you, and let one fly in the air out of fun,
That in only three years, with me hiding me fears, we'd be lined up again, by the Hun.
Oh, we'd joined up real fast, just in case the chance passed, who wouldn't want to be in it?
We drilled and we trained, but excitement soon waned, with bad news from the Front; can we win it?

Fred, I wasn't so sure, but you'd just ignore the doom and the gloom, get stuck in.
Me I went with the tide, hoped, with you by my side, at the end of the day mate, we'd win.
Cobbers eh, Freddy, weren't all staunch and steady, a coupla right mongrels we knew,
"Reckitts" you dubbed 'em, and when Jerry near scrubbed 'em, they turned out quite white in the blue.

"Weak pair of bastards", you said, "they'll both wind up dead", a prediction, which wound up spot on,
Both blown to the khazi outside of Benghazi, and there weren't a lot left, when they'd gone,
We crept in, out of Crete, near dead on our feet, couldn't picture us getting much older,
But you Freddy mate, Oh Jeez you were great, I got scareder, and you just grew bolder.

The terrible two-some they called us, but mate you knew some, if not all of my fears,
Like, late at night when I cried, having dreamt I had died, a secret you kept down the years.
The next few dragged by, it's just in hindsight they fly, and I come back Home, pretty right.
Oh, it's nothing you'd notice, but Jesus don't quote us, see I still wake up bawling at night,

I'm burnt out now of course, what you'd call a spent force, bastard banks took the deeds to the station.
Have we come such a ways, since our Middle East days, when you gave up your life, for this Nation.
I get feelings of guilt, that this country we've built, might of done better with you here than me,
And quite often I wonder if this younger mob understands what it costs to be free.

Am I losing it Fred? Am I better off dead? Seems the world of our youth's, come behind.
Though your body's not near, your spirit is here, it's why I talks to you see, in me mind.
I suppose there's been others, who had better brothers, but no one I've met ever did,
This long life I have led, is down to you Fred, still sleeping in Libya, still a kid.

I'm fading fast Freddy, I think I am ready, to take up where last we left off,
Put the billy on mate, I've not long to wait, got this pain in me chest---bloody cough.

"Come in now please Dad, it makes me so mad, when you're jibbering to old Uncle Fred,
You know he's long gone, gee, you do carry on . . . Oh, Sweet Jesus. my father is dead."

Well you're probably like me and due now for a little light relief. In the interests of multiculturalism I've knocked this one up from a joke I heard in my youth. It remains one of my favourites to this day. Hope you like it. It's called:

How the Orient Express

This is a tale of One Hung Lo, Chinese trader. They're nobody's fools.
I should point out that that was his name and in no way referred to his jewels.
He lived for years in our little town, his neat shop a real treat to attend,
A quiet polite honest family man, most everyone was his friend.
The exception was Nick, a bit mouthy Greek, a hairy purveyor of food
Who ran the café, The Greasy Spoon, who to one and all was plain bloody rude.
Remember those days when each town had a bank? It's hard to believe but a fact.
Well, at the week's end on his way there, Nick would bung on this very cruel act.
He'd call in on One to have his fun and enquire of him, "Chink, what's today?"
And as One would, given his parenthood, inscrutably smiling he'd say,
"It's Flyday, Nick," thinking 'this lousy tlick to play on a man's affliction.
Enjoy it old son,' slyly mused One. 'See, I'm blushing up on my diction.'
Ahh so at last the big day came around. Hung Lo's shop had not seen such a crowd.
Our hirsute Hellenic, all BO and sweat then called for the last time out loud,
"What day of the week is it Chinky Chi?" Said One, "Only peace I seek Nick,
It's Friday, my friend. So let this be the end, but I reckon you still a Gleek Plick."

Written for the occasion of a memorial plaque being placed in Ruth Whitfield Park, Kallangur, Queensland to mark the finding of The AE1.

Found at Last the AE1

So far from her birth at Barrow-in-Furness, she lay asleep,
Our AE1, and thirty-five good men, all buried deep.
Entombed we knew, but knew not where, as for why we know not still.
More than a Century would pass, at last there came the thrill!
We have found her, mixed emotions, a rusting sub, why all the fuss?
It happened all so long ago, well it matters most to us,
And to those who's rellies rallied, when the call to arms was sent.
The Army, Blake Boys, Wal and Fred; To the Navy, Ernie went.
Yet none returned, within a year, three young men had paid the price.
That lets us and ours be here to-day, their lives the sacrifice.
To those dead young men and women, wherever they may lie,
We owe them, we must find them, so we know they did not die.
In vain, far from home and loved ones, we're still searching for some yet.
Our Navy found the AE1, God Bless. Lest We Forget.

Hours before the landing at Gallipoli The Australian Submarine HMAS AE2 threaded The Narrows into the Sea of Marmara to harass The Ottoman Navy. Little has been known or told of this daring foray. One hundred years later a memorial was built and installed in Ruth Whitfield Memorial Park Anzac Avenue Kallangur to honour HMAS AE2 and her crew. This poem was written to try and capture some of the drama and was read at the memorial service. Lest we Forget.

HMAS AE2 The Silent Anzac

Brave are those men who put to sea, yet who are the men who go
Below? Unsure of what may be, these the bravest men I know.
Oh, so short, yet oh so daring was the life of AE2.
First sub to thread The Narrows, Captain Stoker and his crew.

They defied the mines and currents, ship and shore guns, ran amuck,
Blind as bats beneath the surface, it took lots of guts and luck,
But they did it, stirred the possum, bored it up old Johnny Turk,
Guts and luck, that something extra, Aussie teamwork, made it work.

For five brave, grave days, they held them, the Turkish Navy's might.
They submerged when it was daylight, and emerged at night to fight.
They disrupted for a brief spell, shells that fell on Suvla Bay,
They themselves holed in three places, even Sea Dogs have their day.

Captain Stoker gave the order, that all skippers loathe to give,
Abandon ship, Boys, we be scuttled, all hands survived to live
Beneath the Star and Crescent Flag, as prisoners, hard to hold.
For many were the failed escapes, and tragic tales unfold

Of slave labour, hunger, squalor, for these men, three years dragged by,
All grew sick, or felled by fever, lack of treatment saw four die.
Came war's end, repatriation, back to Aussie, home at last.
But for these tired silent Anzacs, their brave deeds had been surpassed

By losses on the Western Front, the killing fields of France.
They are overdue this honour, though belated, here's our chance,
To recognize their sacrifice, made, one hundred years ago,
For brave are those who put to sea, and the bravest go below.

Many men aspire to greatness, yet it favours very few,
You've achieved it, we salute you, Captain, Crew of AE2. Lest We Forget.

This is a romantic little poem for those who are old of body but young of heart and maybe serves as a kind of reminder for those who can't remember. It's called:

Saying Grace is Saying Thank You

Slow and shuffling, they entered my surgery and she self-consciously stated their case,
"We're concerned by the fact that our conjugal act might be startin' to drop off the pace."
Drop off the pace? I thought in amazement for this couple were both getting on!
In years, I should add, they were older than Dad and his 80th birthday had gone!

I explained, "It's a natural progression. The urges that drive you grow weak."
Quite undeterred as if she'd not heard a word, she asked, "Can you watch our technique?"
"Can I watch your technique!" I responded which they obviously took to mean yes,
For they grinned at each other, granddad and grandmother and swiftly began to undress.

I admit I was shocked, the door quickly locked. Now disrobed, they climbed onto my couch
And whatever their age, they knew how to rage with great passion – for that I can vouch!
When the deed it was done, I just stood there stunned, embarrassed and bathed in cold sweat.
Then I said to that pair "My dears, I declare, you're the best two I've seen at it yet!"

Smiling sweetly at that, Gran then slowly began to put herself back in her dress,
"Why thank you, kind man. We hoped you'd understand but there's something we wish to confess.
"We're not married, you see, my dear Cedric and me, by the way my close friends call me Grace.
With my partner long dead now I only have Ced but he loves me, why that look on his face!

We now live in a Home. This's a rare chance to roam but you know there's no privacy there.
Oh we kiss and we pet. This was our first chance yet to be close and to show that we care.
"I forget, did I mention we're both on a pension and can't rent a room they're too dear!
This place is quite nice with a hint of Old Spice. May I please bring my Cedric back here?"

Well, what would you say? They'd just made my day and who in the hell were they hurtin'?
So my answer was, "Yes." Grace whispered, "God bless and we'll see you next week, that's for certain."
So they pop in at noon to play love's old sweet tune and I go to the park for a break.
The year has flown fast. We know it can't last but I pray that it does for their sake.

And while ever they can, then I'll be their man with an hour to myself on those days.
Huh, sure makes life worthwhile and I can't help but smile just knowin' that Medicare pays!
They don't visit me now but I know somehow they've gone to that far greener place.
Locked in memory, I see dear old Cedric as he embraces sweet loveable Grace.

I adapted this from a story about a Cherokee Chief's advice to his Grandson, when asked to explain the meaning of Life. I liked it. I hope you do too.

A Tale of Two Wolves

"You have two wolves, deep inside you, and they're bunging on a blue,
They are ripping, tearing, fighting, cos one wants control of you.
There's the bad one and he's evil, angry, jealous, full of hate,
He's a bully and a liar, you don't want to know him, mate.

"And the other's full of kindness, generosity and truth,
There's peace, love, hope, humility, boy I'm sounding soppy, struth,
I'm so sorry, son." "No, Grandad, this is stuff I really need.
But who wins?" he asked me softly. I replied, 'The one you feed."

Written for the flight business, "Balloons over Brisbane".

A Birthday over Brisbane

Oh, I thought I knew Brisbane, but saw nothing at all,
Til I hung high above it, with Captain Will Paul.
In this big wicker basket, below, his balloon,
Sixty years for my first flight, I'll be back here soon.

Oh so gentle the take off and beguiling the ride,
As up, up and away o'er leafed suburbs we glide,
And so peaceful their passing, one thinks "I'm a bird,"
Just the oohs and the ahhs and the burner is heard.

As the new day is dawning, below us I see
All the hurry and scurry of people like me.
Not to-day though; I'm special, not one of the crowd,
For I'm drifting and dreaming, I'm kissing a cloud.

It's a gift from my children, the best I've had yet,
It's a most pleasant present, I'll not soon forget.
Oh this feeling, uplifting, we're having a ball,
With *Balloons over Brisbane*, and Captain Will Paul.

Freddy, a Prince of a Frog

Young Freddy the frog's feeling frisky,
He'll require female company soon.
He rings Syd the Psychic to find what's in store,
And the news puts him over the moon.

"A beautiful girl, lies in waiting,
She'll show interest in all that you are.
There's travel ahead for you, Freddy.
Leave the pond, and I'm sure you'll go far.

She's caring and gentle, and thoughtful,
Any test you may give her, she'll pass."
"So where will I meet her, this Angel?
What the hell's her Biology Class?"

I believe there's a lot to be said for honesty in a relationship as this anecdote will illustrate. Trust is another matter, entirely.

Banking on a Friend
It's rare these days, an open bank, so we pushed in through the door.
There were only two blokes standing, all the rest lay on the floor.
The man who seemed to be in charge, wore a stocking on his head.
I almost said, fishnets don't work, but I shut me mouth instead,
Cos his right hand held a cannon, well it looked that big to me.
It could disembowel a camel, sink large ships far out at sea.
"You two, up against that wall, keep those arms and legs well spread,"
He mumbled. I feel sheepish. I thought, good onya ANZ.

Then he grabs this teller feller and starts in to acting mean.
I could tell he wasn't too bad, cos them bags they stuffed were green.
Our eco-friendly robber, then proposed we take a stroll,
The wife and I, the teller, seems we're hostages, how droll.
Bit like being in a movie, but of course we're bloody not,
And once outside, our director why he clean forgot the plot.
Removes the stocking, asks the teller, "would you know me again?"
The teller nods agreement, so he shot him in the brain.

At maths I lagged a little, but sum up situations good.
I said, "I'm sure I wouldn't know you, mate, but I think the missus would".

Paddy's Lament.

This new Colleen, I've been dating, I tink she may be the one,
Awful pretty and she's caring, and she likes a bit of fun.
She went off to work this morning, me, I'm in her knickers drawer,
Which I usually find exciting, but the tings in there I saw!

There's a skimpy French Maids outfit, and a Nurses veil and frock,
A lady policeman's uniform,' Saints preserve us, a mock Glock.
I despair I'm disappointed, just as sad as sad can be,
For if Colleen can't hold down a job, she's not the girl for me!

I Wonder

Before settling on the F word, I've wondered what they used,
To register fear, hurt, surprise, or be generally abused.
My research, became Biblical. It was there I found out that,
To cover all those options, seems, they bellowed out, begat.

When Dave first saw Goliath, he yelled to his girl Suzie,
Begat the story, I want gory, fetch a bloody Uzi.
It's never told, the Ark was holed, and Noah roared in a rage.
Keep them begatting woodpeckers in their begatting cage.

But it's a begatting nuisance to have to write this way,
You see three syllables are awkward, I'll take two any day.
I notice some are fidgeting, some talking, there's a cough,
It appears I've lost the Christians, so I best be begatting off.
Thank you.

Birds of a Feather

I've been retired near twenty years, seems ten or more I've spent,
Standing, twitching, bitching, waiting, outside shops, in which she went,
With a cry of, "Just a quick look, won't be long." Well, l flaming hell,
She's got no idea of quick at all, see, as far as I can tell.

See, when quick look's hooked to shopping, and it's of the female kind,
That's when time gets more elastic, at least in the shopper's mind.
Read for quick, maybe forever, it could be an hour or more,
And I am the goose who's waiting, as she ducks in through the door.

Or a quick look, that an echo? Payback from those days gone by,
When I'd leave her minding children as I'd dash out with a cry,
Darls I won't be long I promise, I have had a shave and tub,
I am meeting Blue and Sandy, for a quick one down the pub.

Yeah, in hindsight, could be justice, like the turning of the worm,
So I'll try to stop my whinging, luck with that, I'll stand and squirm.
I'll smile while waiting for My Lady, and gives thanks for what I've got,
Cos though she's still a real good looker, she never tends to spend a lot.

We'd only come to town because the wife had an appointment with this Irish Dr Colin O'Scopy or some such name. I guessed he was Irish cos he'd booked us in for 6.30 in the morning. The dragon behind the counter was as happy as I was to be up and about at such a weird hour. I didn't listen too well what she had to say but caught I had to be back at 9am to pick up Glenny as the procedure would make her disoriented and unable to drive. I was gunna say something but thought discretion was the better part of valour. I wandered across the road to one of them big shopping centre places for breakfast and this is what happened. I called it

Break of Day the Westfield Way

Ate an egg and bacon muffin, taste, epitome of nuffin,
So I'm rolling me a cigarette, which I'll smoke outside, of course.
It is seven in the morning; a winter's day is barely dawning,
When this old boy sandshoes past me, the old girl chasing him: big horse.

I thinks lamb unto the slaughter, then I spots they've bottled water.
Then a mob of them rush by me, my eyes widen with surprise.
Penny drops: she's not a stalker, see her shirt reads, *Westfield Walker*.
Seems they gather here each morning, to partake of exercise.

Well, my first response is laughter, then I work out what they're after,
They seek fitness and the friendship, from the people that they meets.
And though some are quite good lookers, I'd bet none of them are hookers,
And even if they were, I s'pose, this keep's 'em off the streets.

Now this is new to me, not seen, in the places I have been,
And I ponders and I marvels; at the wonder of it all.
This heavy breathing, seething mass, some exuding toxic gas,
And sweat drops for mops of cleaners, whoosh, they thunder through the Mall.

And I hear the pitter patter of their feet above the chatter,
And while most of them are smiling, others grimace in their pain.
Are they high-speed window shopping, or just afraid of copping,
The idea youth has passed them by, and will not come again.

Oh, they're here, all shapes and sizes, no doubt speeding their demises,
Or perhaps past lack of yakka, may have added to their woes.
If you've never put the work in, then it seems to me you're shirking,
And I wonder, just how many, can identify with those?

They all seem in such a hurry, have I reason now to worry?
Am I missing out on something in my home, far from the sea?
But when I go in search of facts, turns out most had heart attacks,
And their Doctors have prescribed this as some kind of therapy.

They surge towards me, then they're gone. How long's this been going on?
As they jostle for positions, elbows pumping, shove and push,
I'm reminded, this is city, living, isn't it a pity?
That they can't all come back with me, and get a life, out in the Bush.

I wrote this one for the Australian Italian Festival in Ingham, thought I'd better have something ethnic. Sweated buckets and had nightmares of little old ladies in black dresses carrying stilettoes that weren't shoes attacking me. Lucky for me they all loved it. Hope you do. If you get a chance to go to that festival held in May, go. It's a ripper. Forgive the accent. They did.

Luigi

Our new priest is young, progressive, he holds seminars and things,
And waffles on a lot about the joy long marriage brings.
Some may question his perspective, on what he has not tried,
But it's he, with the authority, and he'll not be denied.

He said, "Luigi, you've been wed, for nearly fifty years,
Please tell these young folk, how it's done and help allay their fears."
"OK. my young Maria, bella, she so pretty, and so hot,
We go at it like rabbits, yeah, we do it quite a lot.

And the presents that I give her, from her fingers, diamonds drip.
Then after twenty years, I take her home to Naples for a trip."
"Luigi, you are one good man, to treat your wife so well,
So what 's your plan for fifty years, your secret please, pray tell."

"Padre, it no be easy, to keep the marriage on the track,
To-night I fly to Italy and this time I'll bring her back."

Historical Background: Cavemen smelt like men should: Rotten. Sheilas not that flash either. Thus Talc, Snuff, Smelly Frenchmen invented Eau de toilette, (big seller in English-speaking countries, not) . . . then:

The Deodorant Stick

My missus said, "You're on the nose, phew, smell'd make a vulture sick,
Go have a bath and burn those clothes, take this deodorant stick."
Deodorant stick, deodorant stick, not seen one of them before.
Thought, I wonder how you use this? as I closed the bathhouse door.

Well we blokes, we read instructions, on new products, if they've got 'em,
What I read, filled me with dread, "Remove cap and push up bottom."
Well, I've never ever owned a cap, so thought I'll skip that bit,
As for the other, brother, struggle, but eventually it fit.
Snugly; this act, then resulted in, a somewhat tightened gait,
But now, when I'm blowing in the wind, that wind I blow, smells great.

I often wondered what becomes of man's best friends when their working lives are over, especially when trained in the more modern specialised fields.

Fido, my Friend

Throughout History, Legend, Fable, since Man first crawled from the bog,
They've assisted, helped where able, they are man's best friend, The Dog.

Our first was not a retiree, dropout guide dog for the blind,
In looks he was a Labrador, but possessed a Greyhound's mind.
He'd chase cats and rats and rabbits, once he even chased a bull.
He was useless as a guide dog, but the mongrel had some pull.
Rang a mate up in Alaska, where of course the Husky's God,
Crossed his best bitch with our Hopeless, litter won Iditarod.

Our Daughter brought a Beagle home, ex Customs, what a rotter,
No matter where I hid my stash, he'd find it, bloody Squatter.
Our son, his Mother's pride and joy, he, the one I must not hurt,
Whose genes are hers, My Darling Boy I describe as unalert.
Adopts this Bloodhound, Sergeant Drool, ex cop, who'll spot a crim.
He waltzes in, wees on my leg, then points and sez, "that's him".

Then we got an ex Cadaver Dog, but we didn't think that through,
You see, they do the opposite, of what most dogs'll do.
Normal dogs, their bones they'll bury, tend to do that from a pup,
But Cadaver dogs are tricky, see, they're trained to dig 'em up.
We had called our new dog Digger, with his past that seemed quite apt.
He'd attack the ground with vigour, three-foot holes where ere he crapped,

Uncle Dougie loved our Digger. When Doug died, did Digger mourn?
He didn't, dug old Dougie up, they're out playing on the lawn.
Well this caused us much disruption, cos our family's forced to shift,
Our home adjoins the Cemetery, so I think you'll get my drift.

I've lately heard of Rescue Dogs, what the hell's that all about,
If you're tempted, skip retrievers, cos you can't throw nuffin out
For too long; they'll track and fetch it, lay it proudly at your feet,
Sit and grin, their tail awagging, with their paw out for a treat.

No, bugger it, dogs break your heart, I'm up to here with that,
Though I loathe the sneaky bastards, think I'll get myself a cat!

My wife is a great fan of the TV show, Escape to the Country, set in the UK. No doubt forgetting we did it here, 50 years ago, with little knowledge and less money. This incident has lingered long in my Hurt File.

The Worst Two Hundred Dollars I Never Saved

We're a month out from the suburbs, on our little rural plot.
I had never heard of Groundsel, Council wrote, 'Sir, on your lot,
There's a Noxious Infestation, contravening, by law 9,
Eradicate in thirty days, blah, blah blah, or cop a fine.'

Well, great welcome to the district, seems PR's not their long suit.
Second option is, they'll fix it, cost 200 dollars, shoot.
We can't raise 200 nuffins, got a new house, two young kids,
If one of us is out of work, we'll wind up on the skids.

I am thirty, broke and dirty on this Shire without a heart.
With shrubs to clear, this pioneer, had better make a start.
Down the back of our two acres, s'where Obnoxious made its stand,
Groundsel Genocide my mission, brand new cane knife in my hand.

Was I over optimistic, or a young know-nuffin knob?
Dressed in singlet, boots and stubbies, which were not up to the job
Of protecting me from hazards I had not foreseen at all.
Just two strokes, found me invited to, The Paper Wasp Nest Ball.

Holy Moses, aren't they busy, they're aggressive angry, hurt.
Both me eyes are quickly closing, shoulda worn a long-sleeved shirt.
Dance around like drunken Yeti, please stop biting me, I beg,
Slashing, waving my machete, I could lose an arm or leg,

I'm now blind, old Blue's no guide dog, great companion, little help,
His nose must have copped a hiding, by his loud departing yelp.
Just remembered there's an old well, my instructions, fill that in,
I don't wanna be found drowned here, being slack's no mortal sin.

I escape to find the fence line, they all follow venting spleen.
Just last week I ran barbed wire, where the number 8 had been.
Hell's handrail has helped me house-ward, wife's ducked out, goose, home alone,
Bleeding stumps that once were fingers, try to dial unhelpful phone.

Four wrong numbers till I got work, said, I won't be in and why.
Which they all found most amusing, I hang up, I try to cry.
Later, family gather round me, gently tending wounded bits.
Think I can't see silent giggling, but I can through healing slits.

Neighbours visit, smirk and whisper that "he's not up to the task,
Old Dave sprays for next to nuffin, all he had to do was ask."
I resolved then, through the drama, all my pain and my despair,
Should they hold another Wasp Nest Ball, bet your life I won't be there.

Sadly, the subject of this personal attack, did exist; his passing and the method used are unfortunately purely a figment of my imagination. To prove a week in hospital can be inspirational, from my Darker Side comes . . .

Murder, He Wrote

Four old men, all grey and grumpy, atmosphere was whinge and wind,
Only three of us amigos, and the fourth, I felt, had sinned.
I'm the only one half-mobile, vertigo-go on a crutch,
I am also bored half witless, keen to help, but not too much.
I've done random acts of kindness, in my time, but none of late,
Come to think of it, the last one was in nineteen eighty-eight.

Them were days, I was more social, "How's she going mate?" I'd say,
Tip me hat and sorta grin like, but that all turned sour the day
I met – let's call him Horrie Zontal, he could sue me, I suppose.
Know the type? They're always bleating, you shove diamonds up their nose,
Are they grateful? No, just whingers, crying, tears'd fill a glass,
I've re-thought, where I could 've shoved 'em, Satan loves it, me, I pass.

Horrie looks a real bad colour, shoulda carked it years ago.
See, I don't know that he knows that, not just crook, but bloody slow.
'Bout now you think, I'm awful, does this bloke have no compassion?
I've got empathy in buckets; he just overdrew his ration.
With: I'd say "G'day, Good morning." Through his mask he'd gasp, "It's not."
Or I'd say, "Bit colder last night." He'd reply, "I'm bloody hot."

I would ask, "You want the blinds drawn? Lights shine in, it could get cool."
"No; don't you know I'm claustrophobic, are yer deaf, I'm hot, you fool."
Comes two-thirty in the morning, "Oi You, you awake, you mind,
There's lights shining in, they're glary, come here now and fix the blind.
No, back a bit, not right across, I can't stand to feel closed in."
You'll be closed in, in yer coffin, I am thinking with a grin.

Back in bed I am defrosting, four a.m. is not too old,
"Oi, still awake? Close the window now, my feet are getting cold."
Ahh, your feet are getting cold eh, through the window wafts a breeze,
If I ignore his rude request, maybe all of him'll freeze.
Though my thoughts have grown unchristian, window's closed, the blind is drawn,
I am sleep deprived, demented, heard a voice, I could have sworn.

Was some power outside my body, who or what I know not, still
Say, "Son, scrub that sixth commandment, you have my permission: kill."
Can I now sense, some see my side, that I'm not the badder bloke?
Those who've been here, those who've done this, know this bloke deserves to croak.
That, for him, freezing's too friendly, that he warrants suffering; pain.
Should there be reincarnation, would we want him back again?

No: These rubber gloves, are handy, fingerprints won't bring me down,
As across the floor I'm floating. Death stalks in a backless gown.
Oxy hose lays like liana, bringing life to he who sleeps.
Table wheels have stopped that caper. It's a gift, I play for keeps.
Play for keeps, hide panic button, why not? Lose 'em all the time,
I am pumped up, homicidal, could this be the perfect crime?

Play for keeps, and stop creeps breathing, gladly; this to be his lot.
He's down there, where lights are glary, won't be happy that he's hot.
So I'm back to being social, "How she going, mate?" I say,
Tip me hat and sorta grin like, never let 'em ruin yer day.
Just remember, as you travel on, toward your death from birth,
Do try not to be more difficult than those around you think you're worth.

Cheap Flights. Honesty Don't Pay
I was fiddling with the thingo, which I haven't mastered yet,
All I know is I'm the curser, when I'm on the internet.
Then the room filled with her perfume, just a towel hid her delights.
When she asked me what I'm doing, I said "Searching for cheap flights."
I'd not seen her behaving in the manner that she did.
I'm not lying, comes on Cougar, like she wants another kid.
Never ever shown such passion, muttered ja da dore,
Like the mounting yard at Randwick, she's now got me on the floor.
Ripping tearing at me clothing, I grew fearful for me parts,
But her lust soon turned to loathing.
"Whoa, whoa," says I. "These cheap flights are for me darts."

Cuckoo Land
It is not for me I write this, for my time is running out.
It is not that I'm a Christian, more your atheist, devout,
But I shall not, will not, cannot sit in silence, hold my tongue,
While our weak-kneed politicians steal the future from our young.

Maybe this is retribution for the way we claimed this land,
Maybe soon we'll know the horrors that First Nations understand.
We've had migrants in their millions, and I'm grateful I am one,
And we came and integrated, made our home here in the sun.

Took the oath, for we were thankful, tilled the soil, obeyed your laws,
Practised our religions quietly, sent our children off to wars,
Built a nation to be proud of, well I was, but just of late,
I detect a shift in thinking, and it all comes down to hate.

When they tell you that they hate you, how much clearer can they be?
Why bend backwards to befriend them, why invite them home to tea?
Get a grip, you're with the pixies, we don't need them, you are wrong.
What we need are law abiders, folks who fit in, get along.

Folks who have a sense of humour, something this crowd seem to lack,
"Oh! they don't have much to laugh at," neither do our mob Outback.
But they do, cos they're Australian, suck it up and get it done.
Some were migrants, they adapted, found their place here, in the sun.

Don't dare let them Come the Cuckoo, drop their bad eggs in our nest,
If they loathe our laws and lifestyle, where they come from suits 'em best.

Back When
Years ago when we were younger, and we never had much dough,
When bread and dripping staved off hunger, no doubt some of you would know
About five finger discounts, when into a shop you'd lob
To purchase rations for a week, on a budget of two bob.

You'd come home with ten potatoes, carrots, cabbage, hunk of cheese,
Three loaves of bread, a dozen eggs, shirt weighed down past your knees.
Dear old Mum would ask no questions, probably thought that it was free.
Course them camera things have buggered that, and I'm often on TV.

Dog Food Diet
Growing old not over wealthy, but I've lots of time to spend,
My sarcasm gets more healthy, as I slide towards the end.
It appears I can't resist it, should the bait be there, I bite,
And this one, I'll have to list it, though I know it isn't right.

Had this great big bag of dog food, in the checkout line at Coles,
This old Lady, probably my age, Got to love us, bless our souls.
When she asked me, quite politely, "have you got a doggy son?"
I was tempted, no, a camel, but I figured that's not done.

Still the nasty buried in me chose to rear its ugly head,
This dark impulse, it took over, sadly this is what it said,
"It's The Dog Food Nugget Diet, I am trying it again,
I had dropped three stone, the last time 'til I wound up racked with pain,

In ICU with tubes and things, in orifice and nose,
These nuggets are nutritional, fill the pockets in me clothes,
I just nibble when I'm hungry." (I embellish as I go,
By now the queue are all enthralled, I am putting on a show).

Old Granny's hooked yet horrified, "Did the dog food make you sick?"
I'm now flying with my lying, kick it up another click,
"No! I saw an on-heat Corgi, and I thought I'd try my luck,
So I crossed the road to orgy, and I never saw the truck."

Bloke behind Gran roared with laughter, then fell flat out on his back,
No doubt aided and abetted by his massive heart attack.
This has caused Coles stores to ban me, but the coffee shop is fine,
Where I share a cappuccino, with this brand-new friend of mine.

Dear old Gran knows I am lying, but she's lonely just like me,
But she sez a sense of humour keeps her young, besides, it's free.

When Irish ears aren't smiling
In the drawer, to be sure there's knives sharper, I'm referring of course to Malone,
In our village with so many idjuts, Pat does stupid like no one I've known.
He turned up at The Doc's, both ears crispy, looked like bacon that's cooked far too long,
Left Doc in no doubt that he'd have to shout, if he were to find out, what went wrong.
"I was doing me ironing, this morning, the right sleeve of me Sunday best shirt,
When the phone rang without any warning, no one answered but Jesus it hurt."
Doc sez, "Pat, I can see how that happened, but both ears. Son, makes no sense at all,"
"Used my left hand to flatten the other, when I thought I'll give Mother a call!"

Let's put some fun in funeral ads
Ever upward costs are rising, not just living, there's demising.
You drop dead, it's quite surprising, to stop breathing costs a lot.
We all know that Death's unhealthy, affects both the poor and wealthy,
They say our home, we'll have to sell, see,
They want everything we've got.

They fake concern, "How are you faring?" method actors, "let's do caring",
Think of all the loot they're sharing. "Check his eyes, two pennies, coins."
So I've been reincarnated, I found heaven over rated, I'm back to get you blokes I've hated,
You Grave Robbers, gird your loins.

I'll undercut you undertakers, I'll expose you grief-filled fakers,
Make you wish you'd met, your makers; hit you where it hurts; your purse.
So I've launched, The Happy Reaper, we're not grim we're fun and cheaper.
What's that? the ute, bit of a heap, er, s'not a prob, Cobs, that's the hearse.

No love, that's mist, no it's not raining, no you're no trouble, keep complaining.
(I know which part, she is a pain in) If you insist, I'll buy a tarp.
A nice blue one'll, match his eyes, yeah notice things like that, surprise,
I took a punt, not brown, all lies, struth this Sheila , don't half harp.

Well, while we're fixing his dispatching, what got him, got her, was catching,
Two for one, both coffins matching, outside the box, think; get ahead.
So we're expanding, our luck's turning, now do burying and burning.
Stuffed some up, yeah we're still learning, you bet your Life, mate, they're all dead.

Of course, we've had some bad things happen, we said he's dead, they claimed, he's napping,
Which explained the frantic tapping, 'til we bunged him in the fridge.
So, if you or yours are thinking dying, give us a go, you know we're trying.
We'll even toss in, Free Canned Crying.
You Ring The Reaper, Happy, Cheaper, Aussie Owned and Ridgy Didge.

What are you here after? I know
Enough is enough, so I'm keen,
To leave this old world, where I've been.
I intend to go off in
A glass sided coffin,
Thus, my future remains to be seen.

The RFDS (Donations required)

It don't matter what, your colour, creed,
If you are crook, and in real need,
You get in touch, to you they'll speed,
Them Royal Flying Doctors.

It don't matter you're hooked on a horn,
The ute has rolled, an arm is gone,
A Mum's in trouble, baby born,
They're there, them Flying Doctors.

It don't matter where, from Bush or Coast,
For Saint or sinner, Holy Ghost,
They'll tend to all, but you the most,
Them Royal Flying Doctors.

It don't matter why, some things go wrong,
They cry, they grieve, they move along,
They get knocked down, but they grow strong,
Them Royal Flying Doctors.

It don't matter where, look up above,
Grey sky or blue, protective glove,
For you and me; they care and love,
Them Royal Flying Doctors.

It don't matter, when, that hat comes past
Our next deep breath may be our last,
So put in big, and put in fast,
For them Royal Flying Doctors.

Israel

Whether touring Israel, Palestine,
You are walking a very fine line.
For those roads Jesus strode,
Anytime, may explode
With loud shouts of, "It's yours." No, is mine.

Perspectives

When our grand kid was much younger, and the Daughter not too fit,
We would try to help out where we could, you know, do our little bit.
Sam would drop Kate off at Kindy, and I'd get her at day's end,
And I thought I grew less grumpy, and sweet Kate more like a friend.

The Flu found me, I'd a week off, and the missus took me place,
And she'd come home every tea time with this smug smile on her face.
I kind of sensed they were conspiring, Secret Women's Business, eh.
But what about I'd not a clue, until on Saturday.

I asked Kate who she'd rather pick her up, her Gran or me,
When they looked at one another, they could not contain their glee.
Katie giggled, Gran was laughing, giggling. Kate began to speak,
Gran saw no dipsticks, dropkicks, arseholes, though she bets you'll see 'em all, next week.

An old letter written to a Publican and his response. I now know him to be Paul Nielsen, mine host at The Tatts Hotel in Winton., Queensland.

Hotel Letter

Dear Sir,
We wish to stop at your hotel, we will book in for a week,
If you can only grant me, the permission that I seek
To allow my dog to stay with me, each evening, in my room.
Though I realise I'm biased, he is well behaved and groomed.
He's the only family I have left, we're sad if we're alone.
We have planned to leave the thirteenth, can you let me know by phone?

He rang back, and said,
"Mate, I've run pubs for many years, and I cannot recall
One dog stealing sheets or towels or pictures off the wall.
And I've never had to bounce one in the middle of the night,
For being drunk, disorderly, and bunging on a fight.
And mate, no dog ever bolted, with his hotel bill still due,
So if your furry friend'll vouch for you, why you'll be welcome too."

You just cannot protect some people from their own importance, and in this case why would you want to. Thanks for trying.

Mad with the Power

There are good and bad folks everywhere, but that's really no excuse
For the Federal Public Service to have turned this zealot loose.
"I'm from Water Conservation, here's my card. I'm authorised
To assess your allocation, and you'd be well advised
To co-operate completely, for I'll tolerate no quibbling.
And woe betide you Sir, I say, should I detect pipes dribbling.

"Whooa, mate," said the farmer, "you're full on, but give that field a miss."
"What, are you some kind of imbecile? Please gaze once more at this.
"This Sir's my authority, I told you that before,
To do anything, go anywhere, I can't explain it more."
The old farmer shrugs his shoulders, and bids Gunga Din, G'day,
Who then enters No Go paddock and power-walks away.

The Serenity's soon shattered, snorts and screams, hoofs, pounding feet,
A large bull pursues the Know It All who's beating the retreat.
The leak seeker's losing fluids, and running for his life,
Just two steps in front of Ferdinand, who wants him for a wife.
The old farmer climbs the fence and yells, "Mate, if you can't make this yard,
You stop and tell him Son what you told me, and show him your bloody card."

Ambition and Capability

The sign outside the Blacksmith's Shop, read; "Farrier Required."
The homing Paddy, wobbly pinned, with Guinness grin inquired,
"This Farrier chap you're seeking, what exactly, be he doing?"
The Smithy said, "It's simple, he be doing the horse shoeing."
"Horse shoeing, eh, horse shoeing, well, begorra and begob,
I once said, piss off to a donkey, do you tink I'm the man for the job."

This next one could be sensitive to some, but then again they probably won't get it, we'll give it a burl.

Ventriloquy

I was taught to earn my living, sitting on my Grandad's knee,
It was out in Western Queensland, where I learned ventriloquy.
Out there they all can do it, but it's not recognised as such,
They rarely, speak, and when they do, their lips don't move that much.
Close mouthed, I think you'd call them, with their squinting Winton eyes,
Brought on, I'm sure by nothing more than them pesky little flies.

Still I took my skill and honed it, learnt to talk, yet shut my mouth.
We worked Townsville, Brisbane, Gold Coast, then we ventured further south.
And the crowds they seemed to love us, they'd queue hours to see our act.
Oh, have I mentioned little Fred? He gets quite upset, in fact.
It was probably his attitude that brought us both undone,
The smart-mouthed little bugger who I'd raised much like a son.

We was working in some Workers Club, where the lights and life were low.
My subtle stuff's too clever, I was wond'ring where to go.
Then it struck me, do me blonde jokes, they'll go over like a treat,
When this great big fair-haired sheila, she rears up, stands on her seat.
She is angry and articulate, quite incensed, it's plain to see.
"Who on earth gives you the right, Sir, to make fun of girls like me?
To judge people by hair colour, is insensitive at best,
And helps perpetuate the myth, Sir, we're less able than the rest,
Which is false as well you know, Sir, so pray denigrate no more.
Your humour is abysmal, and your presentation poor."

'Struth, I'm copping quite a bagging and I'm feeling guilty too,
So I start to rise, apologise, seems the proper thing to do.
But the blonde who'd only paused for breath said, "you sit down old chap,
With you I have no axe to grind, it's that loudmouth on your lap."

The Painted Horse

He had struggled as an artist, had the gift but lacked the flair,
He'd tried Portraits, Landscape, Wildlife. As it turned out this was where,
Out of nowhere came the answer, as luck mostly does, of course,
When shifty eyes, his newfound friend, asked, "Can you paint a horse?"

"Can I paint a horse? No problem, animals are my forte,
Paint birds and frogs and cats and dogs, Landscapes, do your face, O.K."
"No don't want a bloody picture, you can keep your flaming art,
Want a grey one to be chestnut, and I need it for next start."

Money mentioned, choke the subject, and as beggars cannot choose,
Started in, with brush and roller, piece of cake nothing to lose.
Seems he ran him in a maiden, if he won, next year go back,
As a maiden and a grey horse, threw the stewards right off track.

They suspected something fishy, as the duo split the spoils,
And he copped a lovely earner, for his masterpiece in oils.
But If you're tempted, stick to oil paint, water based can bring you pain.
When they're pounding down the home straight, should it then decide to rain.

The Pillars

No roll of drums, no big parades, no fame or fortune, accolades,
No Icons, Legends, what comes next? They're seldom twittered, rarely text.
They run our shops, The Op and Tuck, if they're your kin, well, half your luck,
Run Soup Kitchens, and Service Clubs, they'll fight in fires, but rarely pubs,
They're S.E.S, they're Ambos, Police, They're ADF, they keep the peace,
They may be paid or volunteers, I'll pull up there, could go for years.
What Life throws up, they sit the test, they try to be their very best,
With helping hand, and loving touch, make time to care, it don't take much,
The point my friends, I'm trying to make, as people go, these take the cake.
They could be old, they maybe young, salt of the earth, Heroes Unsung.
You know who you are, give yourselves a big hug. And thank you from all of us.

Railway? What Railway?

Down South they reckon Queenslanders, are well, different, sorta slow,
And I used to say that's bulldust, but just lately, I dunno.
See, it's come to my attention, back in 1895
We were gunna build a railway. Have you seen a train arrive?
No: We're not slow, we're comatose, of that you can be sure,
That's not even the last century, it's the bloody one before.

What's that, What am I on about? which railway do I mean?
It's The Petrie-Redcliffe Rail link, the one nobody's seen.
When first planned, it was from North Pine; Petrie then, did not exist,
Bit like this phantom railway, I hope the reader has not missed.
The narrator is not happy. Do you feel cheesed off, as well?
If within this transport corridor, your family choose to dwell.

More roads just mean, more vehicles, we witness that each day,
Public Transport's more than buses, what we need's a permanent way.
Each train, eight hundred people, twenty buses off the road,
And how many cars, I wonder? one or two their average load.
They have the land, they have the need, but do they have the will?
This infrastructure's vital, who has the guts to pass the Bill.

This project's history is not pleasant, forked tongues much to the fore,
These electorates have had enough, they will not stand for more.
Each aspirant to represent, must sign an MOU
To kick start this urgent rail link, and see the trains come through,
So let's be better late than never, and in 2009,
Show, if not smart, we can be clever, and build this railway line.

(The railway was finally built 120 years late and opened in 2016).

The Interview
See our Firm required a Sales Rep, the selection's up to me,
A routine and simple matter, yes, but how wrong can you be?
By far the best, most qualified, be a shoo-in one would think,
Was encumbered with a facial tic, a fearsome flaming blink.

His right eye the offender, and I found it disconcerting,
Had he been another gender, I would reckon she was flirting.
But he claimed, "It's not a problem, that two aspirin make it stop."
He starts hunting through his pockets for the pills he has to pop.

First up, out comes his handkerchief, then much to my surprise,
There are all these bloody condoms, I cannot believe my eyes.
Varied colours, types and flavours, the significance of which,
Though I'm well past their use by date, give me an urge to itch.

He finds his pills, his eye stands still, "There, now have I got the job?"
I said, "Son I can't, I'm sorry see we're a sorta close-knit mob,
We can't have a womanizer, which these condoms tend to show,
And although I'd love to hire you, I'm afraid you'll have to go."

He shoulders slumped, then up he jumped, "No, no, that is not true,
I have a wife and family, please let me explain to you.
You have noticed my affliction, but did you ever pause to think,
You try buying Aspirin, in a Chemist's, when you're burdened with this wink!"

Glorious to Behold
We are blessed with natural beauty, within this Shire of ours,
From Bay's edge, up through the valleys to Mount Glorious that towers
High above us, ever vigilant, the sentinel who's brief
Is to guard our prized possessions, every tree, each plant, each leaf.
And all God's living creatures, be they great or be they small
Are subjected to this watchfulness, Mount Glorious sees it all.

It has witnessed tribal gatherings, in days of long ago,
Heard the roaring of the North Pine before they dammed its flow.
Heard the ring of cutter's axes, as the cedars groaned and fell,
Watched the earth fiercely erupting, as they quarried towards hell.
Seen the silver war birds taking wing aloft from Strathpine's Field,
Watched the dairy cattle wander to the sheds, their milk to yield.

Heard the creaking of the wagons, to the bullocks' plodding pace,
Watched the first trains cross this country 'ere further North they'd race.
What went before's now history, for the pioneers are gone.
We know they did what they had to do, but we must now move on,
And we as the new "enlightened tribe" will be held up to account,
So let's hope they learnt a lesson from this sermon from the Mount.

We know what hurts this country in which we choose to live.
We've had the time to diagnose, and the treatment we must give.
Can never make it pristine, but may halt the downward slide,
And keep, this Region, Moreton Bay, a great place to reside.

Our family are close

My mean Auntie Jean married a Jock.
For each Christmas she'd knit me a sock.
For my Birthday, her brother
Would send me the other.
We're tight-knit and tight-arsed are our flock.

Parenting

You walk in a teen-age bedroom,
And find clothes filed F for flung.
That's when you realise you empathise
With those who eat their young!

There's Something in the Air

Way up there in northern New South Wales, where normal's sometimes strange,
You'll find folks are even fickler out around that Nightcap Range.
Dunno why they named it Nightcap, Jeez they'd drink all bloody day.
Well they used to, 'til the sixties, when they found a better way.

Here where rugged rocky ramparts rise, o'er creeks both ferned and mossed,
Lies the village, Bringyerbongalong, in The Valley of the Lost.
Not lost as "where the hell are we?" more like "Hey man, what's going down?"
I arrived impressed, they under dressed and you couldn't find a frown.

I'm in a café called *The Mushroom*, on a toadstool painted pink.
The lights were low, the patrons high, on what, I cannot think,
We shared a smoke and no one spoke, it passed from hand to hand,
Try as I may, I couldn't say, no way could I pick the brand.

It's lo-cal baccy, someone drawled as my eyes began to dim,
And as I grew vague, thought Jenny Craig might use this stuff to slim,
Lo-Cal, great name, but just the same how from this could she profit?
Ahh, her ad might read, "Your face can't feed, especially when your off it."

I kinda drifted off 'bout then, for an hour, a week, a day,
And when I came 'round, seems a friend I'd found, who said "G'day, I'm Ray."
He was sorta short, said he liked a snort, and lived up in the hills.
I was quick to pick that he was sick, always searching for his pills.

He bitched and itched and often twitched and was blessed with just one eye.
This beady orb he fixed me with and claimed, "I was born to fly."
I thought lack of hygiene caused his itch, the twitch I couldn't pick,
But the fullish moon then proved a boon, this bloke's a lunatic.

My one-eyed friend, peered pirate-like to see how I'd respond
To his recent declaration that he sought to go beyond
The realms of earthbound mortals and seek solace in the sky.
I felt I'd better humour him, so asked, "Just how you gunna fly?"

"Well you've seen them flash new glider things, them one's you hang below.
Well I posted off the dough for one, they're DIY you know.
Seems you don't need no licence, not that that bothers me,
I've knocked it altogether, I'll launch meself then I'll be free.

"Oh, I'll need a hand, you understand, for the climb is hard and rough,
But with your aid we'll make the grade, you fly second. Fair enough?"
Up and up we went, 'twas a fierce ascent, to a ledge lodged in the clouds,
And he didn't half skite, about his kite, I near stalled when he mentioned shrouds.

As I strapped him in, gave a dopey grin, then he hurtled off into space.
Ah, it's with me yet, I'll not soon forget, that rapturous look on his face.
He dropped straight out of sight, I thought, "There goes my flight!" then he's back, and he grinned.
He gives me the forks, then he rose like them storks, high in the sky, it's his wind.

Ah with such laissez faire Raymond flew through the air, his face was a picture serene,
But far down below, what we could not know was how cruelly fate would intervene.
For Ma's favourite chooks now wore angelic looks, caused by raptors who bore them aloft.
And it stuck in Paw's craw that she acted so sore and was claiming that he had gone soft.

So when down though the Cumulus Nimbus, with a dive and a climb and a yaw,
Came the biggest bloody meanest eagle that Paw's old eyes ever saw,
He ups with his Under and Over, Yes, Ma's hero once more he would be,
And he shredded big bird at least by a third, and old Ray spent four days up a tree.

Now way up there in northern NSW where normal's sometimes strange,
One word never heard is hangliding, least not round that Nightcap Range.
Oh yes, I still yearn to have me turn, but I'm in no great rush to die.
And should I ever take wing, you can bet on one thing, it won't be where them Wedgetails fly.

I Didn't Wanna

I was born, bit out of Wedlock, run down house on Pearshape Street.
Mum and us six runny-nosers made our family complete.
And of course, we had a Father, but we didn't have him long,
Cutting timber, in the ranges, when it sadly all went wrong.

Well the sawmill said, "We're sorry," and paid Mum what Dad was due,
Back then weren't no Widow's Pension, so we joined the needy queue.
About then I'm re-invented, as I went from boy to man,
Don't recall that I consented, but seems Mother had a plan.

"As the eldest," she informed me, "you must take your Father's role."
But I didn't really wanna, then she said, "God rest his soul."
And though still, I didn't wanna, she was cunning, looking back,
Guilt she built and played my conscience, kept our family on the track.

Chooks and rabbits kept us going; things not nailed down, they were mine.
Turned fourteen, I'm in the sawmill, piss poor wages, but we're fine.
Clawed my way up through the process, tailored in and tailored out,
Sharpened saws, and worked the office, learnt what Life was all about.

Brothers, sisters went to high school, two to Uni, I'm the dill.
One a lawyer, an accountant, pretty soon we owned that Mill.
Mum taught us love and loyalty, what we are we got from her,
Said, "I didn't wanna either; Son, that's just the way things were."

The Procedure or Overreaction

My Proctologist, Rex Bottoms; yes, that truly is his name.
I suspect he changed by deed-poll, you know name to suit your game.
He had huge and hairy fingers, knuckles like a baby's fist,
Should those digits dive inside you, make your eyeballs tend to twist.

He's a wicked sense of humour, but I think he crossed the line,
When I asked, "Where do I hang my pants?" and he said, "Next to mine!"
No way was I warming to him, in fact was growing colder,
When he said, "Tell me how that feels." I'd a hand on either shoulder!

But was just his mate, Ben Dover, yes another smart-assed Doc.
They're both rolling 'round in stitches, while I'm into after shock.
Then I copped it: Home Invasion, log jammed in a rubber glove,
Did I rise to that occasion, I'm now naked high above,

A slowly circling ceiling fan, hung below. Doc Rexy speaks,
He's been dragged there by those fingers, he had plunged between my cheeks,
"If you could just relax your sphincter a trifle, Mr Best,
I'll drop down and write my notes up and conclude your prostate test."

This happened!

Lost Luggage

I never ever saw my suitcase on that airport carousel.
Then the sheila in lost luggage turned my nightmare into hell.
She was big, a Dominator type that eats their young alive,
She sez, "I am a trained professional, now, when will you arrive?"

I just stood there, staring blankly . . . this is much the way, I stood.
"I've been here five bloody hours." She sez, "Now we're getting somewhere, good."
"When will I arrive? I'm here you twit, it's my luggage that is lost."
"No need to shout," sez Nasty Knickers. "Or you'll rue our paths have crossed."

"You're too late," I scream. "That's history, I hated you when we first met."
"Don't underestimate your loathing, we've a way to travel yet."
"Not without my bloody suitcase, or some cash to buy some clothes."
"It could not have cost much money to buy awful clothes like those."

I said, "How come you're in lost luggage, you insensitive fat cow?"
She said, "I'm not, I'm PR Lady, the lost-luggage girl come now.
You are lucky, she's my daughter, taught her everything I know,
And I've a Masters in Discretion, I think now, good time to go."

So she left me with her daughter, I thought, how'd this kid survive?
The answer clear, these words I hear, "I am a trained professional, now when will you arrive?"

Grief comes in many forms, some irrational, most illogical. Self-pity, anger, self-loathing, guilt, sad, happy, past, present, rarely any future, all mixed up to try to make some sense out of our loss. I don't think it ever does.

You Just Dunno

Barely three month since we sold up, living here on edge, in town,
You could hardly call this living, constant traffic gets you down.
Gets you down, it drives you crazy, humming, drumming, day and night.
Our old bush place looking hazy, homesick, nothing here's gone right.

It was sickness brought us down here, we're for better, we're for worse.
Ballroom dancers, never Spanish, this can't happen, you're a nurse.
Always caring, always pretty, soft, as gentle as a dove.
Yes, I know you hate the city, please forgive me, Dot, my love.

I'm so sorry, should have listened, should have stayed home, not come here.
Oh, you swore that it was hopeless, I reacted out of fear.
But the fear was mine, of losing you, so selfish, so insane,
Should have let you do the choosing, where to let go so much pain.

Not down here where no one knows you, lots of Doctors, flaming Hell,
Same old option, softer landing, couldn't fix you, make you well.
Fifty years ago last Friday was when we first tied the knot,
Every day from here's a cry day, I'm no good without you, Dot.

Couldn't give you kids you longed for, wouldn't let me feel no guilt,
Ever caring, never blaming, on such love our marriage built.
Dorothy, when I first met her, didn't last long, 'Call me Dot,'
Wildest dreams I'll not find better, God she's lovely, got the lot.

Come on, mate, and get your boots on, there are folk up home who care.
Friends and patients, waiting, grieving, pack it in, we'll take her there.
Take her back where we first started, promised her, I'll keep her trust.
Be together, won't be parted, she'll be ashes, I'll be dust.

Oh, I dunno about what's coming, after life and all that stuff,
But these fifty years I loved you, Dear, were nowhere near, enough.

Roses Are Blooming, Why Pick on Me?

I'll always treasure those short years we shared, of wedded bliss,
Those living, laughing, loving days, each second breath, we'd kiss.
We revealed in our youthfulness, we touched each other's hearts,
She showed me things that I'd not seen, I'll not forget those parts.

Then I joined the Merchant Navy, in hindsight, a mistake,
Each parting such a tearful time, I feared our hearts would break.
So to pledge my troth, each Friday, to her a rose I'd send.
Oh foolish, foolish, foolish me, to think a bloom could mend
A broken heart, forgive me folks, it's here I tend to choke.
Feel free to scoff, see she took off with that Interflora bloke.

Well that turned me right off florists, and a life spent out at sea.
I went off women for a while, till I met my sweet Mimi.
Still dreamt of someone of my own, someone to have and hold,
Someone special I could care for, throughout life as we grew old.
Then Mimi came into my world, it is true love is blind,
I thought Mimi was her lovely name, but it was her state of mind.

It was "me, me this and buy me that, get out. you're in my space.
"If you really truly loved me, you'd have servants for this place
Which is ghastly, horrid, awful, and it smells, it's so run down.
I want, no I demand, you sell it, and we move in to town."
So I put it on the market, tried to sell, but not too hard,
See, I'd worried that they'd find her, where she was resting in the yard.

When they'd ask me, "where is Mimi?" I'd say she's left me, gone away,
Down South to be a potter, no doubt she'll find herself in clay.
Found my next wife, on the rebound, came complete with Persian cat.
When it scratched me, then I scratched it, shallow grave took care of that,
Underneath a struggling choko, didn't take long, what a sight,
It grew faster than Jack's Beanstalk, luscious chokoes overnight.

Led me musing, back to Mimi. No. I hadn't lost the plot,
I could tell where she was resting, cos the grass grows there a lot.
And this triggered something primal, had a kind of mental lapse,
Beat the council to the roadkill, neighbours' pets fill all me traps.
When Cat Woman knots her knickers, a solution must be found,
And my tiny mind is thinking, she'd fertilise a lot of ground.

And her end was quite poetic, she loved her garden and her sleep.
So I popped her in a flower-bed, dug at night, and fairly deep.
With necessity the Mother of Invention, as they say,
And my wife no longer working, I must find another way.
So went back to Tafe and studied, topped the course, I knew the score,
Graduated with Distinction as a Marriage Counsellor.

And the Garden so prolific, bit like Eden, food abounds,
Flog it off at Farmers' Markets, each weekend I do the rounds.
My stuff's pricey but I sell out, the other vendors panic,
So I tell 'em, lift yer game boys, and get certified organic.

Afterthought . . . So you think I sound psychotic, well I prob'ly am, my friend,
Should you look at our World Leaders, seems I'm following a trend.

The Queue

There's an etiquette to queueing we acquired, back in our youth.
Today's young ones pushy, shoving, they're impatient, that's the truth.
We were lined up, early opening, for we oldies up at Coles.
Nearly seven, from the carpark, comes this young bloke, boldy strolls
To the queue's head, we don't think so. Old Nell hooks him with her cane
Round his neck and pulled him backwards, trips him, he cries out in pain.
Rights himself, then surges forward, he's determined that's for sure.
Poor Old Punchy, who hears bells ring, then left hooked him to the floor.
Where he lay and stared, bewildered, what he said, hard to ignore,
"I'm Tom, your new Coles Manager, let me open up my store."

John Albert Best born 1938 Kent England, migrated 1948. Educated Wilston State School, Brisbane Grammar,
RAAF School of Technical Training Wagga Wagga.
Served 15 years Armament Fitter RAAF discharged 1969.
Various Jobs never settled.
Retired 1998 from Queensland Transport Department.
Married to Glenys 1966 two daughters, Samantha and Kylie.
Worked with People with a Disability and wrote "What's Fair".
Picked up by Access Arts and toured in Cabaret Erratica Melbourne Fringe, Canberra Arts Festival and NIDA
for World Congress on Disability.
Joined North Pine Bush Poets Group Inc.
Won Waltzing Matilda Competition at Winton in 2003
and went to National Cowboy Poetry Gathering Elko Nevada.
Performed regularly various venues around country,
slowing down, lately.
Not brilliant but worth a look.

Ciao for now
Long John.